D1198734

# THE LEGEND OF HUMMEL PARK

## PARK

AND OTHER STORIES

# THE LEGEND OF HUMMEL
# PARK
### AND OTHER STORIES

JEREMY MORONG, WORDS

JILL DAVIS LEBLANC, ILLUSTRATIONS

THE LEGEND OF HUMMEL PARK AND OTHER STORIES

First Edition


Published by 88 Miles Press 2015

"Upon the Housetop" originally appeared in the Winter 2015 issue of *Midnight Circus* as published by EAB Publishing. It was revised for this edition.

"Ellen & Helen" originally appeared in the 2014 issue of *Hollow Round of Skull*. It was also revised for this edition.

Cover Illustration, Cover Design, and Interior Art by Jill Davis LeBlanc

Editing by AE Stueve

Interior Book Design by Jeremy Morong


ISBN-13: 978-0692518311

ISBN-10: 0692518312

*For Abby*




*To my father and mother — Jill*

**Also by Jeremy Morong**

*The Adventures of Braxton Revere*

*On the Backs of Dragons*

# Contents

# THE LEGEND OF HUMMEL PARK

Damon stood at the apex of a long row of winding stairs, his arms outstretched as if he were Rocky Balboa. Panting, he couldn't resist the urge to brag, if only a little. "187, just like I told you!" he yelled. His voice lacked the authoritative quality he was going for, however; it was strained, wavering from the lung-sapping climb. It was a *lot* of stairs, especially when you took the time to count each one out loud as you ascended.

A teenage girl, brunette and athletic, ignored his playful boasts. She trailed behind by thirty steps or so, lost in her own count. She was taking the time to get it right. Damon shook his head, amused at her thoroughness. He could scarcely see her, for it was past midnight and they were amidst a heavy timber that covered nearly all of Hummel Park, a secluded, hilly park on the north side of Omaha near the Missouri River. But Damon could hear her. "153, 154, 155 . . ."

"13, 73, 88, 99 . . ." Damon shouted. It was a lame trick, and he was ashamed to say he had stolen it from *Home Alone*.

The girl's count stopped. "Shut up," she replied. Her name was Sarah. Like Damon, she was a junior at Benson High School. "You're cheating!"

Damon smiled, resisting the urge to distract her further. He leaned over with his arms on his knees, resting.

Sarah neared the top. "185, 186, 187 . . . 188!"

"No way."

"*Yes, way.* You missed that broken one in the middle again."

"No, I didn't. I counted the broken one. Matter of fact, I counted *three* broken ones!"

"Exactly. There are four! And you missed the one right in the middle."

Damon laughed. "This park is playing tricks on your mind. You know, I bet the spirits from the Indian burial ground are tricking you."

"You think so, do you? All right, come with me," she ordered, pulling Damon by the hand. Damon felt a charge at the contact. Handholding was a long way from making out—which was what their friends Kris and Kylie were doing right now, off in the woods, somewhere—but still, Sarah was holding his hand! It was a good start, especially since this was only their second time hanging out. He didn't mind taking things slowly; besides, surely handholding came before making out? Maybe he'd ask Kris about it later, if he could somehow pry him away from Kylie for two seconds.

Damon shook his head. He was uncertain that what Sarah was doing could even be called *handholding*. It was more like dog walking—she was literally pulling him down a long staircase one step at a time. Still, it was better than nothing. A good deal better; Damon was an expert on *nothing*. Embarrassingly, this was as close as he had ever been to a girl. She looked even more beautiful, with her sparkling green eyes and flowing brown hair; he had spent more time than he'd care to admit admiring her from afar; this was much better. He couldn't help but admire how smooth her hand was, and the smell of her perfume. He was more than happy for her to lead him hand-in-hand, until they stopped at an especially large step about halfway to the bottom. But she continued to lock hands with him, and Damon felt his heart sort of flutter.

The step on which they stood was nearly twice as wide as any of the others around. It was part of a staircase that was long and wide, beginning at the bottom of a river bluff and rising to the crest in a twisting, curvy pattern. Fashioned from misshapen stones cemented together in erratic sizes, they were known citywide as The Morphing Stairs, or the Devil's Staircase, and had been the subject of legends for years in Omaha. People swore up and down that each time you tried to count them, the number would change. Some said it was the work of the devil, and others said it had something to do with a group of Satan worshipers that held their evil rituals in Hummel.

Being an original feature of the park, the stairs had long since fallen into disrepair, with many of the stones crumbling or gone. Given the dilapidated condition, it was easy enough to see why the counts were inconsistent. But Damon knew that didn't stop imaginations from running wild, no doubt stirred up by alcohol or marijuana, which many of the city's teens came to partake in on weekends.

Damon didn't believe the other local legends of Hummel Park, either— and there were a lot. Besides uncountable stairs, there was talk of haunted Indian burial grounds, albino colonies, demented hermits, and tales of racist lynchings by Ku Klux Klan members on the trees that hung over Copper Hollow Road, the park entrance, where the trees remained bent to this day. Some said the ghosts of those victims now haunted Hummel, taking the form of mists or phantom lights.

Nonsense, all of it. Damon knew this well, as he had written about the stories for a paper he had done for his *History of Omaha* class. Most of it could be chalked up to parents trying to scare their kids—a colony of deranged albinos, for example. As for lynchings, they had taken place in Omaha, and they were brutal, but the last one was years before the park and road had even been built. When it came to the stairs, Damon figured that his fellow Omahans simply struggled with counting past 100. As far as the other tales, they were so outlandish they were hardly worth mentioning. Nonetheless, he had dispensed with them one by one in his paper.

Sure, there had been violence at Hummel, stabbings and so forth, and a body or two had been disposed of, but such things happened all over Omaha. Hummel was a beautiful place that had had a few unfortunate incidents. Nothing more.

Then again, Hummel was the only park Damon knew of that had a gate blocking the entrances at sundown.

Damon may not have put any stock in those tales, but he'd hang out in a garbage dump so long as Sarah was there. So when Kris and Kylie had read his paper and said it would be fun to check it out, of course he said yes, even if it was a school night. In fact, that might be better; maybe they'd have the park to themselves. Being here alone could make it frightening; scariest of all, they had even left behind their cell phones . . .

"See?" Sarah said, snapping Damon out of his thoughts. "There are two stairs here. Look close. That one is sort of cut in half, but it's there."

Regrettably, Damon let go of her hand as he crouched to examine the crumbling set of stones. It appeared she was right. There wasn't much left, only ruins, but there was enough. It was a step.

"Looks like you're right," Damon said. "You can't even trust the devil to do anything these days."

"I guess so," Sarah replied, but in a way that indicated she had moved on from the stairs and was thinking of something else—she didn't even crack a smile at his lame joke. Damon looked away from the stairs and rose to his feet, feeling a little saddened by her wandering mind. But when he stood, he was stunned to find that she was thinking about . . . him. Her soft green eyes were waiting for him, almost pleading. It made him both ecstatic and nervous, all at once, and yet he did not know what to do next, so they simply stood in an awkward silence, gazing into each other's eyes. She seemed as anxious as he was, which made it worse. Damon knew what he wanted to do, and he *thought* he knew what Sarah wanted him to do, yet somehow, he couldn't. What if he was bad at it? What if she laughed? Or worse, what if he was totally misreading the signs? *Why does this come so easy for Kris and Kylie? Speaking of . . .*

"Where'd they go?" Damon said, motioning toward the place in the woods where their friends had disappeared, somewhere down below. He was ruining the moment, and knew it, yet he kept going. "I haven't heard them in a while." The pleading eyes were no longer asking for him to kiss her; they wanted him to shut up. His hopes circled the drain; the ship had sailed; the train had left the station.

He had blown it.

Sarah paused before answering. The wait was interminable. What was she thinking about? Was she in disbelief over how pathetic he was?

Before Damon could drive himself crazier, she answered. "I haven't heard them, but I'm sure they're fine." She smiled. "I don't hear anything, actually. You know, that's what I like about it here. It's so close to the city, yet it feels so far away. And look up! You can see so many stars through the trees."

Damon did so and sort of smiled. "Do you come here a lot?"

"We used to, when I was a kid. My dad would bring us. He likes hiking and stuff. But it's been a long time. How about you?"

"No, never," Damon replied, smirking. "I guess we were too afraid of the albino colony!"

"Yeah, not to mention the Satanic worshipping cult. You've really gotta watch them!"

"Don't forget Three-Fingered Willie, the mad hermit!"

"Stop before you scare me!" Sarah giggled. "I've never been here at night before—we only came during the day. It does feel kind of haunted, don't you think?"

"Haunted? Not at all," Damon replied, doing his best to play tough. But with impeccably bad timing, he shuddered as a cool autumn breeze swooped down from the trees.

"I saw that," she teased.

"So I'm cold. I'm not afraid of a bunch of pretend albinos, Satanists, or hermits."

"Sure you're not . . ."

"I'm not! It's a bunch of old wives' tales."

"What about all that graffiti in the picnic shelter, the pentagrams and stuff?"

"Big deal. A couple of losers with spray paint. Look at the Morphing Stairs—just a bunch of crap."

"Yet we haven't counted them the same ourselves, have we?"

"All right, all right," Damon replied. "That does it. Let's settle this once and for all. I say there are 187. I *know* I counted that crumbling one."

Sarah smiled. "No you didn't, or you would've counted 188."

"I'll show you."

With that, they returned to the bottom of the stairs, with Damon taking a second to peek into the woods to check on their friends.

"They all right?" Sarah asked.

"For now, but they better be careful. I was wrong about this place being haunted. I forgot about something. Maybe we better go back and tell Kylie and Kris."

"I see," Sarah said, smiling. "And what is it that we should be telling them?"

"You haven't heard? They're making out in a sacred place."

"Oh, really?"

"Yeah, really," Damon returned. "That's where the 1965 Benson Homecoming Queen was murdered."

"You don't say."

"Yep! She was murdered right there. I heard that every October she appears nightly, right at midnight, looking for her old homecoming crown."

"Oh, sure. So she actually wore her crown to the park and lost it? *That* makes sense. Well, what was her name?"

Damon took a deep breath. "Betty Sue, um, McWhatever."

"Betty Sue McWhatever. So she's Irish."

"I guess so," Damon smirked. "I bet if you look closely, you can still see the knife marks on the tree down there. And look at that mist by the parking lot! It's her ghostly apparition, seeking her crown!"

Sarah shook her head, giggling. "Nice try, Damon! Looks like plain old fog to me. If you're trying to scare me, it won't work."

"Oh, I would never try to scare you," Damon said, holding back his grin. "But this *is* a dangerous place. Luckily, I am here to protect you."

"Yes, lucky me! But if you don't let me count those stairs, my protector is going to need protecting! You ready?" Sarah asked, and started counting before he could answer. "One, two, three . . ." When they reached the teens Damon couldn't help himself and interrupted her count until she erupted with laughter and playfully smacked him in the shoulder. They were both tired and bordering on delirious.

Then a strange sound materialized from overhead, ending their laughter. They surveyed the tree canopy for the source. "What was that?" Damon asked, straining to listen as a gust of wind whipped through the trees. But they soon broke out in a new wave of laughter as a "Hoo, hoo, hoo" loudly met their ears. Satisfied that the owl meant them no harm, they shook their heads at their momentary lapse into cowardice.

"I wasn't scared," Damon declared.

"Sure you weren't," Sarah teased.

Damon again turned serious and pressed his fingers to his lips, signaling for Sarah to be quiet. He looked off into the woods, trying his best to search the blackness.

"What's wrong?" Sarah whispered. "Another killer owl?"

"No, something else."

"What?"

"Sounded like footsteps or something. Off in the woods."

"Would you stop trying to scare me, Damon? Next you'll be telling me the famous Hummel Park pack of wild dogs is coming for us, or some other nonsense." At this, Sarah softly elbowed Damon in the stomach.

She was trying to play things off, but Damon sensed she was becoming anxious. He didn't want that. "It was probably a deer or something. Maybe I'm letting this place get to me! Now I'm imagining things."

"Apparently!" Sarah said, her relief evident. "All right, I'm starting over, and don't mess me up this time. And you neither, Mister Owl!" She marched to the bottom of the stairs and began counting, firmly announcing each number as she passed. She gave stair 120, the one in deep decay, an extra bit of emphasis as she stepped on what remained of it. When she finished, it was her turn to stand triumphantly and announce her count: 188.

Damon had kept his distance, knowing better than to interrupt. Despite what he had said, he remained concerned about the footsteps. Sure, it probably was a deer, or some other animal, but what if it wasn't? To make certain, he had casually listened for further noises in the woods. Thankfully, he only heard leaves rustling overhead gently in the breeze. Feeling safer, he picked up the pace and silently made a vow: *no more shy awkwardness.* He was going to kiss Sarah.

She looked beautiful standing atop the stairs, smiling wanly at him. It was now or never. Taking in her smile, he wondered if she knew what he was planning.

Damon returned the smile, but self-consciously; he was trying to play it cool. He had never been comfortable with his smile, cringing when school pictures would arrive, and always praying that he wouldn't look like a dork.

This was not a time for dorkiness.

"I believe you," he declared. "I'm not even going to count them myself. Matter of fact, I'm not counting these steps ever again!"

"Okay, say it then. *There are 188 steps on the Morphing Stairs of Hummel Park. Sarah was right, and I was wrong.* Make sure Kris and Kylie can hear you, wherever they are!"

Damon laughed. "All right, fine." His heavy footsteps pounded on the surface, and he gathered his breath to prepare for a proper public apology. He looked up at Sarah, admiring the silhouette of her athletic figure atop the long stairway. She was active, playing softball, volleyball, and soccer for the school teams, and doing well in all of them. Damon wished he had her athletic ability, but when it came to after-school activities, he was kind of lame: yearbook and German club. That was it.

Lame.

Yet the German club was where he had met Sarah, who was waiting patiently for her apology. Well, she would get it. He would say it loudly and proudly, as soon as he reached the top.

As Damon climbed the stairs, he stumbled over step 120—the broken one. He looked down and tried to regain his footing. But when he looked up, seeking Sarah, he was stunned to find another silhouette joining her. *A man.* He towered over Sarah, a strange outline capped off with what appeared to be a top hat placed crookedly on his head. Whoever he was, Damon knew the man was up to no good.

"Sarah, watch out!" he screamed, his voice cracking. Any pretense of trying to appear cool was dropped.

Sarah heard the warning and threw her arms up, bewildered by Damon's terrified instructions. She lost her balance and fell, but before her knees touched the steps an arm reached out, seizing her around the waist.

The man's powerful grip pulled her close and held her, undaunted by Sarah's flailing arms and legs.

Damon broke for the top of the hill. His legs pumped like they never had before, but as he drew near, he slowed. It wouldn't do any good to play hero. He held his arms up, palms open, unsure of what to do next, and unsure of how to do it even if he did know what to do. He stared at the man's face, concealed in shadows. "Just take it easy. We don't want any trouble," Damon said, doing his best to silence the hammering heart in his chest.

"No, I bet you don't," the man sneered, stepping forward into a pale patch of moonlight. Damon flinched at the strange sight. Their assailant was clad in a worn black leather jacket, over-sized, with bizarre patches and crazily painted symbols adorning it. Damon couldn't be certain but the images on those patches—pentagrams and skulls—seemed Satanic. More, when Damon's eyes adjusted to the faded light, he gasped.

The man was an albino. Damon had never seen one before but he was certain of it. He was African-American, like himself, only it was as if his skin had been bleached a fish belly white.

Were the stories true? It was impossible.

It wasn't that the man was an albino that startled him so, it was that he was an albino in *Hummel Park*. It was an urban legend come to life. Were there more like this man, lurking in the trees and covering the forest? Damon scanned the woods, expecting to be snatched up at any moment.

"That's right, mother fucker," the man said in a hoarse voice while he clamped down harder on Sarah's mouth. She squirmed and her eyes bulged. "I'm part of the colony. You lookin' for me?"

"No, sir," Damon said. "We don't want to bother you. Please, just let her go and we'll be on our way."

"It's not that easy," the man said. "You're trespassin'. This is my home, see? I've been watchin' you, and listenin'. I don't *like* you. You think you're so smart. Still think Hummel's a myth?"

"I am sorry, sir," Damon said. "I was wrong. I believe now. But I wasn't looking to bother anyone. Please, let Sarah go and we won't trespass anymore."

Damon surveyed the forest again, wondering if anything the strange man said was true. And where were their friends, Kris and Kylie? Were they still making out while Sarah was in danger? Or maybe they were getting help?

Wherever they were, Damon couldn't see them. The only sign of life was a light breeze that rippled through the trees. Thinking, Damon nearly fell over as if he had been hit by a thunder bolt—what if this crazed man had already taken care of Kris and Kylie? What if he had killed them?

"Lookin' for help?" the man said in his irritating, scalded cat voice. "You won't find any. It's just *us*. Me, you, her, and Hummel Park."

"Please, sir, let Sarah go and we'll be on our way—"

The man spat. "You're disrespectin' me. You come in here and talk big. You ain't so big now, you piece of shit. What'chu doin' with a nice girl like this Sarah, anyway?" Again he clamped down, her anguished screams muffled by his large hands.

"I'm sorry. I just thought it was all a myth—"

"No myth," the man said. "Goin' to bring all the old tales to life tonight. What were you doin' here? Gettin' wasted? Wantin' to do up a pretty little

white girl?" He ran his fingers through her hair, stopping to smell the ends as they passed under his nose.

"No sir. Nothing like that. We just thought it would be fun."

"Is it? You havin' fun, girl? I bet—" The words disappeared as Sarah managed to break the man's grip. Once free, she contorted her body and spun around so that she was facing him. She reared back and kicked the man between his legs. The man howled; Sarah fled, leaving the stairs behind to dash over the bluff.

Damon watched this play out and saw his chance. Without a second thought he charged, flying up the stairs and leaping in what was his best attempt at a football tackle. He soared through the air and landed hard, his skull colliding with the man's chest. If this had been football, the ball would have spilled into the quarterback's own end zone. The albino fell backwards, his head crashing against stone.

Damon could hardly believe it—the blow had left the man unconscious.

"Go, Sarah," Damon ordered as she watched from the hill. "Run out of here and get to the car."

"What about Kylie and Kris?"

"Crap! I forgot about them."

"Oh my God, Damon, we have to find them."

Together they ran down the stairs, arriving at the parking lot and flat meadow at the bottom that gapped the forest. "Kylie! Kris!" they yelled, their voices shaky. They combed the woods where they had seen them last, but there was no sign of them. Damon shouted as loud as he could, desperately hoping for an answer.

There was no response.

"What if there's more of them?" Sarah panted. "He said there was! What if there's a colony?!"

Damon scoffed. "Bullshit. He's crazy. Still, he's enough to deal with on his own. We better find Kris and Kylie and get the hell out of here." He whirled in a circle, hoping their friends would come staggering out, but he only found trees and overgrown weeds. "Dammit, where are they? They could've gone anywhere!"

Sarah pointed to a narrow game trail they had missed earlier, carved into a section of thick undergrowth. "Let's try this. Maybe they went down here. But I wish we had a flashlight."

Damon took a deep breath. "It's worth a shot."

Damon led the way. They beat around clumps of weeds and brush that grew along the trail, hoping for a sign. It felt so hopeless that Damon could hardly believe when he actually found them. "Oh crap, here they are Sarah!"

Their friends were bound together by rope, leaning against a large oak tree to the side of the trail. Damon and Sarah ran to them. When they arrived, they bent down. The raspy breathing of Kris and Kylie told them they were alive, but no matter how much they shook them, their friends didn't wake. Worse, the well-tied knots wouldn't loosen.

"Damon, I am so freaking scared," Sarah said. "What are we going to do? These ropes won't budge."

"I don't know," Damon replied, his voice weak. "This is insane. Wait, I've got it!" He had found a slack place where he could pry in a finger.

From there, it was easy enough to loosen the ropes and release his friends. They slouched over face-first into the dirt.

Damon took the rope in hand and grit his teeth. "I'll be right back. I better make sure that creep is still there. If he is, I'm tying his ass up."

Sarah tried to plead with him to stay, but Damon pretended not to hear. He knew what he had to do. He would not let this lunatic hurt her, no matter what.

He went down the trail and into the grassy clearing below the stairway. He looked at the empty parking lot and wished someone, somehow, had heard him yell and summoned the police.

Unfortunately, it was all up to him.

He ran to the stairs, took a deep breath, and exhaled. *This was it*. With any luck the crazed lunatic was still out cold. If not, he could be waiting somewhere in the woods, ready to spring out and attack. With that cheerful thought Damon climbed carefully, following the winding path while keeping his eyes focused on his surroundings. When he came to the final turn, he did so breathlessly, hoping that the man would still be there, flat on his back.

But when Damon whipped around the curve, the albino was gone.

"Crap," he said. "Where did that son of a bitch go? Oh no, what if he goes for Sarah again?"

Damon bounded down the stairs, his feet struggling to stay under him as he glided over the shabby staircase. He was dripping sweat when he arrived at the game trail, and wanted to throw up.

When he returned to where he had left Sarah, he felt even worse. Kylie and Kris remained unconscious, and they were bleeding from their heads.

This was a newly inflicted wound; a broken branch lay on the ground next to them.

And Sarah was gone.

"Sarah!" Damon cried, his legs turning to jelly. How had the albino worked so fast? Damon felt completely helpless. Rational thought left him. He turned around in circles, examining the forest as if she might run out from somewhere, safe and sound.

Damon could hardly believe it. Had the albino doubled back and snuck in from behind, creeping through the woods and attacking when Damon had left? Or perhaps there really was a colony in the park, with a tribe assisting this bizarre man?

"Jesus. What the hell do I do?" Beads of stress sweat streamed down his forehead. He was cotton-mouthed, and his hands shook. He tried again to rouse his friends; Kylie only mumbled, and Kris drooled. Neither would awaken. Damon held his head in his hands, wanting to cry, wanting to scream, wanting to run anywhere so long as he wasn't here, and might have done so if it wasn't for one thing: Sarah.

Damon stood up, pissed off. He was going to find this man, or else.

But the man had found him. He stood underneath a low hanging tree branch twenty feet away, staring at Damon, holding a sickle as if he was the Grim Reaper himself. Blood dripped from the blade.

Sarah's blood. Had to be. Damon felt faint, and threw up.

"Look at you. You're a pussy," the man spat. "Haven't you ever heard what a bad idea it is for black boys to come to Hummel Park? Are you retarded, boy?"

"Screw you, man! Where's Sarah!"

"Sarah learned her lesson. She won't be coming here with no black boys no more."

"You're black!"

"The hell I am," the man shot back. Drool hung from his chin, which he wiped clean with the sleeve of his coat. "I'm as white as you can get. You blind, boy?"

"You're still black."

"If you say so. It don't much matter. I don't fit nowhere, except here. But we can talk on the way. You come with me." He held up the sickle, the message clear. In case it was not, the man spelled it out. "If you do, I promise I won't kill you with this. I've got a gun, too, but don't wanna use it. Guns bring attention. I don't want attention yet, so don't make me!"

"Screw you!"

The man spat again. "You're a feisty one. But I'll make you a deal. You come with me and I won't hurt your little girl anymore. But you've got to come with me, or its sickle time."

Damon took a deep breath. He wanted to throw up again. It was insane to go along with this maniac, but he couldn't see another way. If Sarah was alive, Damon had to keep her that way.

"All right," he muttered. He knew he wasn't thinking clearly, but if he cooperated then maybe Sarah would be safe, along with Kris and Kylie. He only needed to keep this guy distracted long enough for them to come to and escape.

"That's a good boy. Real good. Now we can talk. See?" The man spit again. Damon wasn't certain, but he thought his attacker was every bit as nervous as he was. Before the thought could take root any further, the man continued. "See, you say I'm black. My parents were, so I guess I am. But you know what people used to call me?"

"No clue," Damon said, "And I don't care. Where's Sarah? I want to see her and know that she's safe. Then I'll go with you."

"Screw Sarah! This is about me and you! Don't worry about your white bitch. She's just fine. Real fine. She won't bother us; she run off. Guess she didn't like me much. But never mind her. I got a lot to say. Important things. Now walk, or else I find Sarah, and stick this sickle in, and maybe somethin' else, too!"

Damon reeled at the horrid words. *Ignore them*, he told himself. *They're only words. He just wants to get a rise out of me.* "All right, I'm coming with you. Whatever you say. Just let my friends go home safe."

"I ain't gonna harm another hair on those crackers' heads. Besides, they won't do no good to ole Catfish dead. I need 'em alive. Now move."

Damon did as he was told. The man led him forward, waving the sickle back and forth ominously as he did. Together their feet crunched on fallen leaves as they marched across the parking lot and onto the road. "Catfish? Is that your name or something?"

"That's what I was tryin' to tell you. They all called me Catfish. Black boys like you, especially."

"Why?"

"Look at me! Look at my skin!"

"I don't get it."

"All right, looky here. See, we went fishin' one time and I pulled up a big ass catfish, whiskers and everything. Beautiful fish. Biggest one anyone ever pulled from that lagoon. I know it was. They all said it, even the old-timers. But you know what some of 'em said? Kids who was supposed to be my friends? They said 'look at the belly on that fish! Why, it's snow white, just like you!' And from then on everyone called me *Catfish*. I hated it at first, but by and by I didn't mind. I kind of like it. What's a name, anyway? Don't mean nothin'. Say, what's your name boy?"

"Damon," he said. He remembered hearing once, on TV most likely, that you should humanize yourself in a hostage situation. He'd give it a shot. "I'm in the 11ᵗʰ grade. I go to Benson High School. I live with my mom, my dad, my brother, and—"

"I don't give a fuck," Catfish barked. "11ᵗʰ grade, huh? You take Omaha history yet?"

"Yes, sir. Taking it this year."

"That so? I bet you flunked, dumbass, or you wouldn't have come here," Catfish said, pressing the wooden end of the sickle handle into Damon's spine. "You need to bone up on your history, boy. I heard you talkin'. You mentioned albinos, and hermits, and Satan worshipers. Well, I'm all three. See, it's all true! But you forgot one. Maybe you didn't want to talk about it around that nice little white girl. You ever hear what they used to do to black boys here?"

"Yeah, I heard. They say that racists and crap would lynch people, and that's why the trees lean over the road. But it's all bullshit. I read about it. Copper Hollow Road wasn't even *there* when people were getting lynched."

"Good! You do know somethin'! You ain't as stupid as I thought, maybe. But don't stop now. What else you know? Me, I know all about Hummel Park. You know why?"

"No, sir—"

"Because I *am* Hummel Park. You won't understand, but I do, and that's enough. See, not a thing happens here unless I let it. There's not a body buried or some punk kid drinkin' his first beer that I don't know about. Saw you assholes come in an hour or so ago, I did. Knew every move you made before I made *mine*."

"Fuck you," Damon growled. He knew it was a mistake, knew he needed to stick to his humanizing strategy, but he was feeling pissed off and the words seemed to escape of their own accord.

"No, fuck you!" Catfish returned, the sickle jabbing Damon's ribs again. "This place is special, yet you came in here like you owned it. Dancin' on *my* staircase. Sickening. Well, this is my home. You wanna know why?"

"Not really."

"Too bad. You're gonna learn it all, now. I was a kid once, a real piece of shit like you. Well, I had been goin' out with a white girl, too. Nice girl. Her dad, not so nice. He came to take us home after a dance. It was just him, her, and me. Made some introductions. He didn't say much, just sort of motioned for me to get in the car.

"I could smell the booze on his breath when I got in. He had one hell of a load on. Well, about halfway home, he flipped out on her for seein' someone like *me*. Then he let me have it, too. All sorts of talk. He slammed on the brakes right there on Pershing Drive and told me to get the hell out and never see his little girl again.

"Once the shock wore off, I noticed that I stood right in front of the sign. You know the one. *Hummel Park*. The old man had taken me home after all. Everyone always said there was an albino colony here. So instead of walkin' to mama, I went lookin' for *them*. My own kind."

"What did you find?" Damon asked. He found himself shaking again—if Catfish did have friends, that would mean trouble for Sarah, Kris, and Kylie.

"Nothin'. Weren't no albinos here. No hobos, either, and the only Satan worshipers I ever come across were a bunch of scared kids who would go runnin' off at any hint of the police. *Pathetic.* The devil would've been embarrassed.

"Now I ain't done. I slept in a picnic shelter that night, right here in the park. My life was forever changed. I knew it right off—Hummel was where I belonged. It needed me. See, when you come down to it, Hummel was a joke. A bunch of stupid stories. But I could change that. I could *matter.* There might not be an albino farm but I'm an albino. And I could be a hermit and a Satanist, too. Why the hell not? God cursed me already. Now I could curse him."

Damon shook his head as they journeyed through the park, passing by the picnic shelter, playground, and bathroom. "So you think because you're here, all of the old legends just spring to life? That you make them so, simple as that?"

"That's right. All the legends of Hummel Park are goin' to come true thanks to me! When people talk about Hummel, I don't want them to make up crap. I want them to *know* there's an albino. I want them to know there's a crazy hermit, and that they can come by to worship the devil with one of their own. I'm givin' Hummel *life.* The life it deserves. I've done a lot, but I've saved one for last. Tonight, it's gonna come true, too."

Damon considered this and could stifle the tears no more; they flowed freely. "I want to go home. Please, let me go. Why are you doing this?"

"I just told you, if you'd listen. Open your ears!" He prodded the sickle into his hostage's back again. "Or I'll open them for you."

"I don't understand!"

"You're an idiot. But you'll learn. Now move!"

Catfish led Damon across the park road and back through heavy underbrush. Poison nettles scraped at Damon's legs and he struggled to stay upright as he tripped over twigs and branches that were strewn about. They began to go down a bluff, a treacherous, steep climb, until they came to a clearing. Catfish motioned for Damon to stop. "Take a look," he ordered.

The winding river road, Pershing Drive, loomed below, lit by sporadic streetlights. There were wide, empty soccer fields and a massive cornfield somewhere below, and beyond those lay the river. The Mormon Bridge that took the interstate from Nebraska to Iowa shined brightly to the south, and there were lights on at the US Coast Guard facility. Downtown was alight off in the distance. Otherwise, all was in darkness.

Damon took this in and tried to think of an escape. He knew there were homes around the park, but they were on the other side, nowhere near close enough to hear him scream. Even if they could, they'd never make it in time. He'd have to find another way.

The bluff on which they stood was another of the unique, fabled features of the park. It was a barren hillside, with a few scraggly weeds here and there, and tree roots that stretched vainly into the dirt only to give up and seek other routes. Growing on this slope was a constant battle against driving rains and the soil erosion they brought.

"Know what this is?" Catfish asked.

"Devil's Slide," Damon said, quietly, as if speaking any louder would summon untold spirits and haunts.

"That's right. Lot of jumpers here. Seen many go myself. Helped 'em along, too, if they lost their nerve. Was glad to do it."

"I'm not jumping."

"No, you got that right. We seen enough of those. Just wanted to introduce you to this place proper-like. It's important you know all about it, see? You gonna be here for a while. You notice how hardly nothin' grows here? You know why that is?"

"Erosion?"

Catfish cackled. "You is stupid, ain't you? *Erosion*. No, you ask me, it's because this is where an Indian graveyard was. They got screwed over by the white man too. As a reminder, they made it so nothin' can grow here. But who knows, really? Just one more of Hummel's mysteries."

"I see."

"Don't talk smart with me," Catfish warned. "I don't like it. Now get your ass goin'. We've got one last place to visit. One last introduction."

The sickle drove the message home yet again, forcing Damon to move. His thoughts again turned to escape. All this talk of last visits and introductions told Damon that the situation was growing more serious. His thoughts ran in countless directions, each plan more complicated than the next, when he forced his mind to stop. Perhaps he was overthinking this. Sure, the man claimed he had a gun, but what if he didn't? Even if he did, he could still make a run for it. If he reached tree cover before the man could fire, he might find safety. Hummel's isolation had been his enemy; perhaps he could make it his friend. He could navigate the timber and make it to one of those houses at the edge of the park, and get help.

Catfish, working as if he had a sixth sense, seemed to understand that Damon was making a plan. Before Damon could take action, a hard blow landed on the back of his head, and Damon slipped into unconsciousness.

When Damon awoke, he did so with a shock. There was something digging into his throat; the pain had jerked him awake. His arms and ankles were bound. His face was pressed into mud. Waves of nausea pumped through him. His head throbbed, and his body was covered in scrapes. Bits of weeds and debris stuck to his clothing. Damon could see that he had been dragged here. But where was *here*, exactly?

He twisted his body and found swaying tree branches overhead, with a clear starry night sky peeking through the branches. The trees bent downward, their branches tangling together, reaching out like outstretched fingers to form an archway. With great effort Damon raised his head, fighting desperately to see with his blurred vision. He was on a hill, which had been carved out years ago in order to create the stretch of road that he knew was winding below.

Damon shivered as it all came clear. He was underneath the hanging trees that draped over Copper Hollow Road.

His head throbbed and his heart pounded harder. He had to escape, somehow.

"Good to see you're awake," a gravelly voice intoned from somewhere Damon couldn't see. It was a voice Damon knew well, now. He wished he could forget it ever existed.

"Why are you doing this?" Damon stammered, coughing. The rope around his neck was choking him; it hurt to talk. He winced, and closed his eyes.

When he opened them, Catfish was there, standing proudly. Damon studied the man and his strange clothing. He was reminded of a clown, a sick version of one of those Shriners that would torment children at parades. His top hat came apart at the seams and allowed white dreadlocks to poke out from the lid. A strange necklace hung from his neck, made of what appeared to be small animal bones. His teeth were rotting, and black, and there was a trickle of blood coming from his nose—*perhaps from Sarah?* Damon wondered. He wished he could add some damage of his own.

"Ain't I explained it already? I would do anything for Hummel," Catfish said, nostrils flaring. "This park gave me a reason to live. Before it, I was nothin'. Just a freak, someone to make fun of. But that's changing. I'll be every kid's nightmare in this stinkin' town. Catfish'll be the reason punks like you come here at night, lookin' for a cheap thrill. They'll find it, and more, won't they? Like you and your friends have.

"See, Hummel Park needed *me* just like I needed it. You were right—it was all bullshit. I already told you what wasn't here—no albino colony, no hermits, no Satan worshippers. Not until me. And you were right about the lynchings. Nobody ever hung from *these* trees. Oh, they lean and sway all right, but not from corpses."

"How the hell do you know?" Damon spat. He was doing what he could to keep Catfish talking. The more he explained, the more time he wasted. Any delay might save his life.

"Oh, *I know*," Catfish replied. "It ain't that hard to figure out. People are dumbasses. Especially you kids. But I hate to disappoint folks. Don't want them to think Hummel is safe, and that little black boys can come here and not get strung up. That ain't right. The world needs a little danger in it, don't you think? So, as promised, tonight the legends of Hummel Park will be fulfilled!" His crooked grin spread across his face, a monstrous look. "We gonna have a black boy hangin' for the first time!"

As he finished, Catfish quickly swung around and peered down the road. Damon thought he might explode with joy; there was a car heading toward them. His chest drummed wildly as the front edge of headlights cut through the night.

Damon and Catfish watched together, breathless.

"Looks like your lucky day," Catfish muttered, putting his hand over Damon's mouth. But as the last word drawled out, the engine quieted. The vehicle slowed. Damon could hear brakes squeal and gears shift, then the familiar whine of a car in reverse.

Just like that, his savior drove off.

"Damn, boy, guess it ain't so lucky after all. Tough break." The fright gave Catfish new urgency. There would be no further delays; the car had doomed Damon. Within seconds, he found himself pulled roughly from the ground; a swift tug on the rope around his neck lurched him upright. The rope pulled tighter until Damon was left to stand on the ends of his toes. He desperately searched for a foothold to keep his feet on the ground and the weight off of his neck.

Catfish tied a stick around the other end of the rope and threw it into the air. It went over one of the leaning branches and looped around, then fell back down to the ground. When it landed, Catfish bent over to retrieve it. "Ready or not, here it comes!" he said, drool dripping from his crooked teeth. "This is for Hummel Park!"

Catfish pulled the rope. Damon felt it squeeze. He thrashed against it. His feet left the earth and swung wildly. He couldn't breathe, couldn't scream. He fought the grip of death, but death fought back, and his vision turned to stars.

Damon spun in circles, twisting at the end of the rope. Down below, in the gleaming moonlight he saw Catfish's horrible visage, the broad, toothy grin growing wider. He could see the sickle on the ground, cast aside. Leaves blew across the road. Low-hanging tree branches seemed to reach out for him, beckoning him to give up and accept death.

"Say, maybe they should call you Catfish instead," his murderer shouted, howling with laughter. "You should see yourself flop around! I'm tempted to throw you back in. Catch and release!"

The tree swayed under his weight. He wished the sagging branch would crack, and tried to put pressure on it, but that only increased the strain on his throat. It was all over. All that was left was for him to die.

He thought of his mom, and how his last time talking to her would be a lie. He had told her he was staying at Kris's house for the night. He had never lied to his mother. He regretted that he had.

Childhood memories flooded back. There were people, faces, and events he hadn't thought of for years. Puzzlingly, he remembered he hadn't finished his edits for his latest yearbook article.

Then he thought of Sarah, and how he had looked forward to coming here with her. In his delusions, brought on by a rapidly fading consciousness, he thought he saw her, floating in the air like some kind of angel. Maybe he was going to meet her. He supposed she would be killed too, or maybe she already had been, he couldn't remember. He wouldn't remember anything, ever again.

The world began to fade when the rope slackened. He felt himself fall, then land with a crash. A shooting pain pulsed through his leg. It was shattered; bone protruded from his right shin. He rolled down the hill, spinning wildly until he came to a stop on the road. Loose gravel rubbed his face raw and gave him road rash. Stunned, he watched as the rope uncoiled from the tree limb, fell, and landed in front of his grateful eyes.

Still more shocking, a top hat landed atop the pile of rope. Damon looked up at Catfish's familiar silhouette, but now the shadow contained the outline of a pole jutting from his back, as if it was growing from his left shoulder. The living embodiment of Hummel Park screamed in anguish.

Damon saw Catfish fight with the embedded pole, trying to wrench it free. But he gave up, as the pain was too much. Again he howled, agonized by both his injury and his failure. He cussed loudly, spun around, and tore up the road, growling, a primal, guttural sound, and never looked back. Damon watched him run away and rejoiced, seeing that Catfish's very own sickle had been driven into his back. The monster disappeared into the forest, a trail of blood dotting the road behind him.

Soon, Damon was even more astounded, as he was looking up at Sarah, beautiful Sarah, with Kris and Kylie behind her. They were safe, somehow, though battered. Sarah was holding a torn piece of cloth to a gash on her neck; Kris and Kylie were both staggered. Sarah's face was stained with tears and her shirt with blood, but she was *alive*. Miracle of miracles, so was Damon. He didn't quite know how, but Sarah had saved him. Sure, Kris and Kylie were there, too, but only barely, knocked woozy from the various beatings they had suffered. He knew it was Sarah. He looked into those green eyes, made ever more beautiful and green by the starlight and her tears, and he knew now he would do what he had vowed to do.

Damon reached up and pulled her down to him, ignoring the shooting pain in his leg. He brought Sarah close and smiled, caring no more if he looked like a dork. It was then, finally, that he had his first kiss, their lips mixing with blood, tears, sweat, dirt, and grime, with Kris and Kylie, for once, having to look on.

# A BURDEN

I didn't know who many of them were, but at the funeral they would pull me close and say, quietly, as if they were going to impart on me some great wisdom, that the Lord never gives a person more than they can bear.

I would smile weakly, nod, accept their embrace, and thank them. Then they would go on their way.

I would think to myself, each time, how terrible must the Lord be if He has fashioned me in a manner that I could withstand such a tragedy?

Then, later on, I was struck by another thought, one that was worse, somehow. I would think to myself, if that was the case, then how terrible must I be?

When I was a child and people would speak of heaven, they said it was a place where we would go and be reunited with our loved ones. This held no sway with me. My loved ones were alive and well, and we were together. I had been fortunate that way. I had lost a cousin, once, but I had only met him at a family reunion and hadn't liked him, as he wouldn't share his toys, of which he had many. I saw no reason to want to join him. Both of my grandfathers were gone, sure, but they had passed before I was born so I did not know them, and was therefore uncertain that they would be waiting. I was fine right where I was, thank you.

Those were childish thoughts. Now, I can only hope my loved ones and I will be reunited.

I was brought in for questioning a few days later, but I thought little of it. I understood. They had a job to do and were exploring all angles. Soon, for the first time, I was forced to entertain the thought that this was not some horrific, tragic accident, but a crime. A *murder.* I had thought, perhaps, that I would never feel alive again, to never touch a human emotion beyond grief, but soon I was ready to explode with great rage and fury. I wanted to know who did it, and why. Once I found out, I wanted to catch that son of a bitch. Make that murderer feel a small piece of what I felt, and impart my hell on *him.*

The questions began to grow harsher as the interview progressed. I thought they were only testing me, doing their due diligence, but it became obvious that it was more than that. Turns out, I was the suspect. It was unfathomable. I could hardly breathe. Imagine, being accused of killing what was most important to me? I grew angry, and lashed out. I made demands. I insulted them. I asked for a lawyer. Through it all, there was one constant. I could not understand how and why this had happened.

Perhaps I made it worse. I don't know. Reason left me. I could not wrap my head around it. I'm no monster. I would never. I wasn't even there. How could they?

I told them the truth. Told them where I was. Told them to check it out, that I had an alibi. Yet they kept coming. The questions never seemed to stop. I did not even have time to answer. They kept hammering away.

*"Admit what you did." "Admit it! You did it!" "If you confess right now, as God as my witness you won't see the chair. But if you stand there and tell me you didn't do it, then I will personally make sure you burn for this." "Own up to what you've done!" "What's this? I see you've got a bit of a history." "Be a man! Stand up for your crime!"*

They kept on. They tried every avenue they could. Anything to make me admit to something I could never do.

*"Was it the money?" "Were they getting in your way?" "Could you just not stand them anymore?" "Problems with the marriage?" "Wanted the life insurance, did you?" "I bet if we ask your mother-in-law, she'd have some stuff to say about you." "Hated being a father, I bet." "Your old lady, was she cheating on you?" "Care to talk about these domestic abuse allegations?" "You were acting pretty strange at the funeral, you know. Almost like you were happy it was done." "What are you going to buy with the money? New car?" "Tell the truth and it'll all work out. But this is your last chance!"*

I'm not ashamed to admit I cried. Oh, I cried. I think anyone would have.

But once I finished crying, I became angry again. How dare they?


I spent that night in a jail cell. The first of many. Five counts of murder one. Said they had all the evidence they'd ever need. Said they couldn't corroborate my alibi. Charged me. Booked me. Took my mug shot. Over, done. I would be left to rot until the trial.

The next morning I met with my lawyer. One on one. No cops around. He said it looked bad. Real bad. I could tell that he believed them. Wouldn't look me in the eyes. He focused on the ground when he advised, in so many words, that I plead guilty and take the offer of life in prison. Said he could still get it for me. Seemed to think that was a big favor. That he'd done something great. Said that given the heinousness of my crimes, it was my only way out. Anything else would see me fry.

I fired my lawyer.

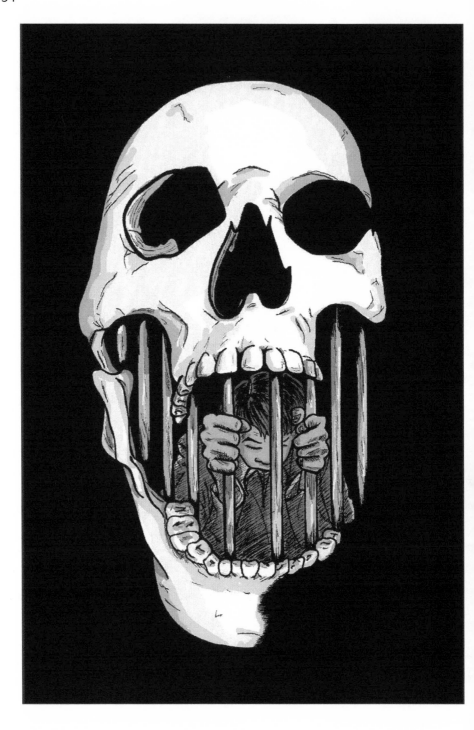

The anger ran its course, and I was broken. I had lost everything. I didn't even want to fight. I was numb. The question wasn't how could I carry on. The question was why would I want to?

You might say that the Lord had given me more than I could bear.

If I only knew that it had just begun.


They placed me in solitary. For my own protection. Keep me safe until they kill me. Sitting there, alone, it gives a man time to think. I needed it.

Eventually, I decided to fight.

This would not stand. I would prove I was innocent. It should have been easy enough. I was.

Met my new lawyer. Told him I planned to appeal. All the way. Young kid. Big case. In each other, we saw opportunity.

I had devised countless ways to kill myself. I cast them aside. The anger I felt was good. It gave me something I had never again expected to possess: the will to live.

I would bear what I had been given.


They brought in a whole team of experts. Arson experts, people in nice suits with perfect haircuts. They spoke in important tones with gravity and sincerity. They talked about char patterns. Burn temperatures. Liquid accelerants. They were all very professional. Good looking. Handsome. Men like me, once.

Very capable, all of them. Yet not one was capable of looking me in the eye.

I went on the stand. Had my day. Finally. I explained it all. Told it just as it had happened. Told how I wasn't there. I told them where I was. I told them who could back it up. I told them how I felt when I arrived at the scene. Told them that just because I might have acted strange and erratic at the scene, that didn't make me guilty.

They said it did.

I lost it. I'd like to know how those sons of bitches would act if they came home and found that their house had burned to the ground with their wife and four children trapped inside? That their entire life was in ashes and ruin?

Took them a little longer than I expected. Not long enough. I knew what that meant. The jurors took their seats. They looked relieved. It had been a long trial. They had been sequestered for weeks. Trapped. Caged. Imprisoned. Freedom was on their minds. Theirs, not mine. Soon, they would be home. I bet it felt good.

They say juries don't look at you if they've found you guilty. It was so. I don't know that I heard the judge say it. *Guilty.* I knew he had said it. I felt him say it. Heard the courtroom exhale. But I never heard the word.

I took it quietly, trying to figure out the way an innocent man was supposed to act when he's been told that they've found him guilty of killing his own family. That he'd be sentenced to death for doing so.

I don't know that there was any such way.

There was one appeal. Then two. Three. Four. I lost count, there were so many. Kid lawyer is a man now. Long gone. New lawyers, same results.

But something has changed. A group has taken up my cause. They believe me. Can't tell you what it feels like to hear that. After all these years, they believe.

This is my chance. All that talk about liquid accelerants and so forth? Bullshit. All of it. Bad science. It wasn't arson. They can prove it.

I've got my own experts, now.

More than that, I have hope.


Hope was fleeting. Turned out, time was up. No more appeals. I used them all. Only one option left. We asked for clemency. We asked the governor. We asked the Board of Pardons and Paroles. Fancy name. They never responded.

It's all over, now. Here I am, sitting in a chair. *The* chair. Strapped down, ready to die for something I did not do.

I can't look at the people who have gathered here as witnesses. Some of them worked hard to keep me out of this chair. Some of them toiled to put me in it. I won't look. I don't know the proper way for an innocent man to appear before midnight strikes.

Midnight means a new day. But not for me.

More experts show up. Execution experts. Strange job. They check the straps. They inspect the connections. Make sure they are good and tight. Double-check. Triple-check. Don't want anything to go wrong. Imagine that.

I can't hold back the tears. I am not angry. I am not anything. I only want my family. I want to feel them. Want to know they are here. But I can't feel.

They put a mask over my head. I look up at the ceiling while it slips over. My world goes black. I take a deep breath and hold it.

They pull the switch.

The Lord gave me more than I could bear.

# UNWANTED

Her office phone's shrill ring snapped Rachel out of her contemplation. It was strange to be called this early. It felt like a violation—the morning was her sanctuary, a time to take a deep breath and brace for the hectic day that would follow. This intrusion was unwelcome, and defeated the purpose of showing up before the day's business began.

She instinctively reached for her Starbucks cup and took a sip while reading the name on the caller ID. She could only smirk and shake her head. *Dad.* Well, she should have seen this coming . . .

In truth, Rachel had expected the call, but not until later in the day, perhaps around lunchtime. She had momentary thoughts of letting it ring to voicemail, but she knew that wouldn't do; she wasn't certain that her father knew how to leave messages. Even if he did, he wouldn't bother— he would hang up, call again, and the phone would resume ringing within seconds. *Resistance was futile.*

She picked up the phone.

"Hello, Dad."

"How did you know it was me?" a confused voice replied.

"Dad, I have caller ID. Most phones do these days."

"Oh, that's right," her father said. Without missing a beat or offering small talk, he moved right to the reason he was calling. "Say, have you found a home for that dog yet?"

Rachel sighed softly. "No, not yet. Like I said, it could take a while. We only dropped him off yesterday, Dad! You know it's hard to find a dog a good home these days."

"All right, all right," her father replied. "Well, you let me know. This little mutt is driving me crazy. I don't know what to do. He keeps staring at me like he wants a walk or something."

"Well, why don't you take him on one? It would do you both some good."

"Harrumph," her father grunted. "You sound like my doctor. Well, maybe I will, before I go insane. But you let me know if you hear anything!"

"I will, Dad," she replied. It was unclear if he had heard her or not, as the next sound was that of the dial tone.

Her phone rang even earlier the next day, catching her before she had left for work. Rachel answered quickly so as not to disturb her sleeping children.

"Hello, Dad," she whispered softly.

"Hello? Can you hear me?"

"Yes, Dad," Rachel replied, whispering louder as she moved to the kitchen, where it was safer to talk.

"Hi Rachel. Any news on this dog?"

"No, nothing yet."

"Well why not?"

"We're trying. We've got the little guy posted on the internet. Someone will want him, but sometimes we have to be creative to make an unwanted dog wanted. It takes time. Especially with an older dog, and a mutt."

"Well, he ain't that old. He's only seven."

"To some people, that's old."

"Well, that's a bunch of crap. Anyway, you let me know when you hear something. I just got up and the fool thing wants me to walk him already!"

"Oh, how can you tell?"

"I can tell. He's driving me crazy, staring at me all the time and trying to sit on my lap. You know, you want my advice, you might be able to get rid of him faster if you'd change his name from Foxy. What a terrible thing to call a boy."

"Well Dad, that's the name he came with. We figure he's been through enough for now. And it doesn't seem to bother him at all."

"Yeah, well, I wouldn't want to be called Foxy, I can tell you that."

With that, he ended the conversation the only way he seemed to know how, which was to hang up the phone.

Over the course of the week, the daily calls continued, and they all went along the same line. When Saturday came, she left her kids with her husband and decided to meet her father for breakfast, taking care to call ahead. When she knocked on the door, she heard the dog bark from inside. "Foxy! Stop it, boy!" came her father's answering shouts. Rachel smiled. It was good that the dog was so loud. It was a nice added benefit. Her father lived in near seclusion, a lonely house on the edge of a large, foreboding park at the edge of the city. It was the way he wanted it.

Still, Rachel worried. Bad things happened in that park. Rapes, stabbings, dead bodies left underneath piles of leaves. There was no telling what else.

Of course, her father hadn't always lived alone. While she waited for her dad to come to the door, she stared at the nameplate on the mailbox— Ed and Christine Davis. Even now, though her mother had been gone for over a year, it was hard to digest. She didn't imagine her dad would ever

update the plate. Which was fine, as Rachel wasn't certain that she wanted him to.

The door opened after her dad's usual struggle with the lock. "Hi, guys," she said to her dad and Foxy, who was wagging his tail next to him.

Her father appeared to be happier than she had seen him for some time. Rachel had to work to hold back a grin.

"Are you here for the dog?" he asked hopefully. A little *too* hopefully. Maybe she was misreading the source of his happiness.

"I'm here for breakfast, Dad—you know that!"

"Yeah, I know, but I thought maybe someone would want him by now. You said this was temporary."

"Yes, that is what I said, but I also said that it could take a while. Many of our dogs stay in their foster homes for some time." She took a deep breath before continuing. "Don't you like Foxy?" She bent over and scratched Foxy's ears. The dog wagged his tail faster.

"Yeah, I like him just fine. He's a fine animal and that's why you should have no problem getting him a home."

"Well, if you like him, Dad, why do you want to get rid of him so fast?"

"Harrumph. I can't get any rest with him around. He wants to walk, and to be fed, and he's always barking at the door."

"At least it gives you something to do, right? I mean, how many reruns can you watch? I think you've seen every *Star Trek* episode 50 times."

His lip curled. "I don't want him getting too attached, and thinking this is his home. It'll make it harder for the next people to take him in."

"It will be fine. It happens all the time. It sucks, but that's how it works." She paused, wanting to say more, but knew there were risks to moving too fast. She had been taking small, cautious steps in the way someone crossing a frozen lake on a warm day would. Perhaps it was time to risk it. "Or maybe he could just stay here with you . . ." She said it quietly, but the slight bit of surprise that registered on his face did not go unnoticed. He had heard her.

"Let's go to breakfast."

Yes, he had heard her, but he was going to ignore her. *Typical.* Feeling that the ground, while slushy, remained firm below her, Rachel decided to continue. "Besides, you're up here all alone in the woods, and God only knows what goes on in that park . . ."

"I'm fine, dear, but I won't be if I don't eat soon. *Breakfast.*"

It wasn't the answer she had been hoping for, by any means.

On the other hand, he hadn't shot her down, either.

***

The daily calls continued for a few weeks, each one coming before she left for work. He was wearing her out and so she had begun avidly searching for another home for Foxy, a permanent one. There were no limits to her dad's stubbornness.

It was Monday, with Rachel waiting in line at Starbucks for her morning coffee, when she was struck by a thought.

Her dad hadn't called.

This wasn't unusual. Before the dog, they would go up to a week without talking. Maybe longer. Of course, that was *before* Foxy. It was strange how quickly a new routine could build in one's life, and how suddenly askew it would feel if there was any deviation.

She resisted the urge to panic. After all, this was a good sign—maybe he was giving in, and he'd keep Foxy. On the other hand, it wasn't like him to give up on something once it was in his head. The way it had been going she figured there was another three or four months of work left in convincing the old man to keep Foxy, and she wasn't sure she could take it.

She took her phone from her purse and pulled up her father in her contacts, unsure if she should call.

*** 

It was early in the morning and Ed was awake already. He was staring at the TV, absorbed in an episode of *Star Trek* he had seen countless times. It was no matter, as it was one of his favorites, the one where Captain Kirk outsmarts a computer so thoroughly that it blows itself up. Staring at Ed was the brown mutt that had been dumped on him, every bit as absorbed in Ed as Ed was in the television. *Foxy*.

"What the hell do you want, mutt?"

The dog cocked his head at Ed's voice, nearly turning it until it was parallel with the ground.

Ed tried his best to ignore the dog's pleas as the computer on TV began to spark and smoke. "All right, all right." Ed pushed his recliner handle down, lowering his feet to the living room's faded brown carpet. The chair creaked as he rose. "Just let me take a leak first. I can't stop at every blade of grass to piss like you."

With the bathroom door shut behind him—he lived alone, sure, but that didn't mean he had to live like a savage—Ed took care of his business. He turned on the faucet and waited for the water to warm in order to wash his hands. While he waited, Foxy started barking. "Shut up, Foxy!" he yelled.

But the dog continued, then began scratching on the door. He hadn't done *that* before. Ed shook his head mournfully. This mutt was starting to get a little too comfortable here.

"Hold your horses," Ed yelled over the pouring water. "I'll be right out, Fox."

If the dog heard him it never let on; if anything, the barking grew more incessant and whiny. Ed turned the faucet off and dried his hands quickly on a towel that was beginning to smell of mildew, muttering under his breath about his daughter's schemes. "What do I need with a dog? I need some peace and calm, that's what I need!"

He shoved the door open and Foxy bounded toward him, his front paws landing on his thighs. Having gotten Ed's attention, the dog ran to a large picture window that overlooked the woods. Ed went over to the dog, picking up the dog's leash on the way. He reached down, grabbed the collar, fastened the leash, and pulled him away from the window. "What's wrong with you, boy?"

Ed gave the dog a scratch on the head and pulled on the leash, but the dog fought him and broke free, leaving Ed to stare at the mutt in bewilderment. The dog was mad, growling, and it was only then that Ed looked out into the early winter darkness.

Ed gasped and nearly fell over in surprise. In the front yard, peering around a tree, there was a man staring back at him, clad in a dark hooded pullover, his features all but concealed by his clothing, the tree, and the lack of light. He had been looking inside through the picture window, stalking Ed's every movement. When Ed spotted him, the watcher turned and ran, darting into the woods, leaving behind the confused homeowner, who was rooted to the unsightly carpet.

Once Ed got his wits about him, he went to the phone to call the police, but his heart sank—there was no dial tone. He slammed the phone down. "Damn phones," he grumbled.

Ed was trapped, with his nearest neighbor two tree-covered blocks away.

Then again, he wasn't completely alone—there was Foxy. Better, there was man's *other* best friend, his gun, a Smith and Wesson, just like the one Dirty Harry carried. It was in his bedside table. He jogged over to his bedroom as fast as his old knees would carry him. He reached out for the drawer, when there was a loud CRASH. Ed fell to the ground, covering himself from shards of breaking glass as his bedroom window shattered. Two arms appeared on the window ledge and soon that creepy face appeared. He was white, with a dirty brown beard that had grown in unevenly. The invader was perspiring heavily, with a dark hood from his jacket pulled overhead. He had the look of some of the panhandlers that Ed would see when he'd meet his daughter for lunch downtown. His pupils were dilated and if Ed wasn't mistaken, he was wasted. He was a junkie.

"Get out of my house!" Ed yelled as the man pulled himself in, scraping his stomach on shards of jagged glass. If the sharp glass hurt him the junkie never let on.

Ed went for the table, but the junkie was too fast. Worse, he was strong, despite his wiry, haunting, skeletal appearance.

They became tangled together, wrestling, Ed going for the drawer, the junkie going for, well, Ed didn't know what, exactly, but he was fighting with a fury. In desperation, Ed wrapped his arms around his attacker's waist, trying to wrestle him down, clenching his teeth as he tried to somehow summon his old strength. But the junkie shook free, and threw Ed off. Ed spun backwards and crashed into his bedpost. He cringed in pain, but it was only beginning. The junkie knocked him down, then pressed his knees into Ed's chest and began pummeling him with sharp quick jabs that connected with jaw, teeth, and nose. Ed felt his nose break and panic overtake him. He writhed and tried to shake the junkie loose. But the junkie only shrugged off the attempt and loaded up to deliver a stiff blow to the side of Ed's head. It landed flush, and left the older man nearly unconscious. In what felt like hours but was less than a minute, Ed was facing his end. The junkie dug into his pants pocket, finding a small pocketknife. It wasn't much of one, but it would do.

The junkie struck, laughing as steel met flesh and blood, the knife stabbing Ed in the stomach. Ed gasped as the attacker reared back for another strike.

***

Foxy had been barking at the window and wouldn't move for nothing. He cared not that the strange man had fled; he'd stalk the front window and bark all day if he had to. This was his house, he was in charge here, and the warning to the stranger was clear: *never come back*. Foxy wasn't having it, not even when the man who lived here tried to pull him away from the window, for some reason, but Foxy broke free and resumed his march.

Foxy filled the air with his yelping until the sound of shattered glass came from the rear bedroom—*his* bedroom, where he had taken to sleeping at the feet of the man. Foxy did not understand what the shattered glass meant, and was hesitant to abandon his forward defense. His ears twitched and his head cocked back and forth as he weighed his next move. It was all so confusing. The stranger had been at the front window, yet here were these other sounds coming from behind him . . .

Then there was a shout from the man. Something about a house. *My house*. With a final look at the big window Foxy turned and sped toward the bedroom.

*** 

Rachel called again and again with no success. It only rang incessantly, and Rachel shook her head at her father—*really, who doesn't have voice mail?* Then again, he had never needed it; he always answered. She couldn't remember a time when he hadn't, though she never understood how, seeing as it was a landline—her dad was many things but he wasn't a hermit, and got out from time to time. She supposed he could be taking Foxy for a walk, but surely he would have been home by now.

Finally, she excused herself from the office and got in her car. She shook her head sadly, wishing she had a way to reach her dad's neighbors. Of course, he didn't really have any . . .

She knew she could call the police and do a well-being check, but somehow, that seemed wrong. If anyone was going to discover her dad, it should be her.

***

The attack had taken mere moments. Already, his foster father was in grave danger. There was no rational thought, no reasoning, no planning—the dog was all action as he charged through the doorway. There was a strange man in the room, leaning over the man that lived here. Foxy knew it was the *stranger* right off; he was the man in the window. Foxy growled; the window man did not belong here.

*This is my house.*

Foxy's paws skidded as he left the carpeted hallway for the polished wood floors of the bedroom. He struggled to maintain control on the slippery surface, contorting his body as his front legs went one way and his rear the other. Off-kilter, he managed to jump on to the bed, never slowing as he ran across the bedspread and leaped, launching himself into the air.

\*\*\*

Ed prepared for the killing blow. The first stabbing had been immeasurably painful, and Ed knew the next one would be the last, if he wasn't dying already. He was no longer in control of his thoughts. For some reason, all he could think of was his mom calling across the neighborhood, shouting loudly so that he could hear where ever he was—in a field, or the creek bed, most likely. Just him and his dog Shadow, catching frogs, tromping through the stream, making forts, climbing trees—well, Ed would climb and Shadow would wait. Ed could hear his mom calling, "EDDIE!" It seemed so real, so genuine, and Ed began to feel that perhaps it was. He wanted to go to it, to answer the call, to make the long walk, just him and Shadow, where they'd both return to find dinner waiting and piping hot. She called again, a little louder, the way she always did when he didn't answer right off. He got ready to call back, "I'm coming, Ma!"

Then there was a scream, ear piercing, terrifying. Ed was home, now, but *his* home, not his mom's. It was that damn junkie, screaming hysterically as he struggled to cover his face. Ed wondered at what could make the junkie react so.

Then he saw Foxy. The dog, that wonderful mutt, was latched on to the junkie's face, refusing to let go until he tore away a swath of flesh from his cheek. The dog lost his grip and thudded to the bedroom floor. He fell sideways, landing on his ribs, but quickly found his footing on the slippery hardwood and prepared for his next attack. Just as he coiled himself to spring, there was a loud BANG. A body fell on top of Foxy, pinning him to the ground.

***

Foxy snarled, snapping his jaws as he tried to free himself. He could tell that the body had stopped breathing. He knew, somehow, that the fight was over. Anxious moments of difficult breathing followed, but Foxy soon felt relief as the crushing weight was lifted from him. The limp body thudded on the floor next to him.

"Atta boy, Foxy," he heard his foster dad gasp while scratching his head. "Atta boy. That's a good dog."

***

When Rachel made it to her father's home, she felt her entire body stiffen. To look at the house from the driveway all appeared well, but she knew better. The house was dark. Asleep. Her father would've never slept so late. She pulled out her phone and made a quick call to 911, then sadly searched her key ring and approached the front door. She opened it, terrified of what awaited.

She was met full-on by the charging Foxy. His hair was unkempt and thick drool coated the fur on his face, but he bounced on his hind legs and gratefully kissed her hands.

Her father soon followed, wincing, staggering down the hall while clutching his ribs. His shirt underneath was stained crimson. His face was washed out, and his breathing ragged, but he was alive.

***

It appeared things were winding down for the day, as some official looking folks came along and put the junkie's body into a vehicle, one that reminded Foxy of the dogcatcher vans he had once worked to avoid.

His foster dad sat in the back of another vehicle, white with flashing lights; a woman in a navy blue shirt was tending to him. His daughter was at his side, giving him one last tearful embrace. Foxy couldn't understand what was being said between the two of them, but they were looking at him, and smiling.

Those smiles, he did understand. They told Foxy that no longer would he have to flee vans such as those currently parked in front of the house, for Foxy was now home.

# ELLEN & HELEN

Ellen kissed her boyfriend good-bye for the umpteenth time. As usual, they refused to end the agony, stretching the process to torturous lengths.

Helen, her sister, squirmed as shivers crawled down her spine. She stifled a gag when the lover's lips smacked together, bile rising at the little kissy noises they made.

She was forced to listen, having no choice in the matter. Her only defense was to turn her head as far as her compromised body would allow, close her eyes, and let the anger rage inside until the suffering passed.

The lovebirds finally finished their bit of unpleasantness. Helen resisted the urge to upchuck along with the stronger, more primal urge to strangle her sister. *How much more of this could she take?*

"Good night, dear," the boyfriend said. A stupid grin spread across his face, which masked the evil intentions that Helen knew lurked behind his every move. He turned to her. "And Helen dear, please think about what we have asked—it would mean so much to us." He grasped Ellen's hand as he said this, very much playing his ridiculous part of one-half of a happy young couple in love.

*Disgusting.*

Helen merely nodded in reply, indicating she would think it over. It was a lie. There was only one thing Helen would be thinking over, the same thought that had consumed her ever since this boyfriend had entered their shared lives.

Then again, she couldn't blame it all on the boyfriend. He had only sped up the process. With or without him, it had been a long time coming.

Helen simply couldn't take anymore. No reasonable person could. Imagine being attached to your sister, always, forever. There was no escape; no refuge. Helen had handled it with grace and patience, but no more. Her sacrifices weren't appreciated; she was unloved; her feelings were ignored.

Things improved little when the boyfriend left. They never did. His exit left Ellen googly-eyed, lost in a fantasy land.

As usual, the sisters sat down to watch television. But did Ellen ask what program her sister might like to watch? Of course not. No, she did what she always did. She turned it to one of the stations—of which there seemed to be many—that was airing that *America's Funniest Videos* show. Helen was convinced that when the world suffered an extinction level event, wiping out all life except the cockroaches, those cockroaches would gather around the warm glow of *America's Funniest Videos*.

Still, it was keeping Ellen occupied, which was exactly what Helen wanted. Helen's eyes were on her phone, her savior in moments like these. Her fingers danced across the touch screen as she searched for ways to refine her plan.

When the program came to an end, Helen cringed. The distraction was over. Ellen's mind was unfettered, and Helen knew what was coming next.

"Have you thought it over, Sister?"

Helen rolled her eyes. "I have, Sister," she replied. She paused, letting the tension build and the hope rise in Ellen; Helen savored it until she brought it all crashing down. "But I don't feel that I am quite ready yet."

Helen knew what was coming next. Tears. Nasty, disgusting, wicked, *beautiful* tears, for Helen wanted her sister to cry, wanted her to despair.

The more she sobbed, the more readily she would agree to the next stage of her plan.

"I will be ready someday soon Ellen, for I know how long you have waited for this, and your boyfriend seems to care for you so! But, you see, it would be rather uncomfortable for me, and I'm not sure you have considered that fully. Nonetheless, I am working on a plan."

"For goodness sake, Sister! I have waited my entire life for this! I am a human being, and here I finally have a boyfriend in this impossible situation. A chance to be my own person for once! Why would you deny me this? Me, who loves you so, Sister!"

Helen sighed, finding it difficult to remain calm. She grew tired of being blamed for impeding her sister's independence when the truth was nothing of the sort. The opposite, in fact.

"Ellen dear, I did not say no, I said *not yet*. Did you not hear me say I was planning something? But surely you can understand why I would be uncomfortable?"

Ellen sniffled back tears. "Of course I understand, Helen. It's just . . . I want it so badly."

"And I want it *for you*, Ellen. It would be a wonderful feeling to act as others do. So much has been denied us due to our situation. And that is why I have come up with a plan. I had hoped to perfect it further, but I can see how eager you are, and, yes, I do believe it is time."

Ellen's eyes grew big, though they were difficult for Helen to see. "So you do have a plan! I thought you were only humoring me. Oh, Sister, what is it? Do tell!"

Helen had her now. The line had been cast, and the bait taken. Now was the time.

"It's really quite simple. I will take a sedative, Sister. Then I will sleep right through, and you will be, for all intents and purposes, completely alone with your boyfriend. Just like other couples! It would be like I wasn't even there when the . . . *act* takes place. How does that sound, Sister?"

Helen could feel Ellen's body jump with excitement. Of course she would be OK with this plan. The burden would be bore solely by Helen, as always.

"What a marvelous idea, Sister!"

"I thought you might like it."

Ellen stretched out her left arm, the only arm she had, and reached out to grasp Helen's hand, the way she always did when she showed affection.

"Sister!" Ellen exclaimed. "This is amazing! And I would do anything for you to make it happen! Anything! Oh, what can I do?"

Helen paused, taking deep breaths and sighing, as if she was reluctant to speak her next words. She took another deep breath and exhaled before finally replying. "Ellen dear, perhaps there is one thing. It seems to me that it would be wise to test the sedative first. Truth be told, I'm a little scared. What if it didn't put me under long enough? It would ruin your lovely moment."

Helen could feel Ellen tense before growing excited again. A plan had come to her. "Oh Helen, why don't you try it on me first? I'm sure it's perfectly safe and then we will know for certain it works!"

A slight grin appeared on Helen's face, try as she might to bury it. She gave up trying. After all, it was of no consequence—Ellen was unable to see her face without the aid of a mirror. "Are you certain, Sister?"

"Of course! I'd be happy to. Then we would know that it works!"

Helen wasted no time, ensuring that Ellen would remain captured by the excitement of the moment. She rocked on the couch and lifted their shared body into a standing position, carrying her sister with her the way she always did. It was the only way. Helen moved directly to a cabinet in the kitchen and retrieved a small bottle. It was the same bottle she had slipped into her purse at the drug store when Ellen wasn't looking, discretely placing it in the cabinet later on.

"I didn't want to tell you about this until I was absolutely certain it was the right thing to do, Ellen. But you have convinced me."

Helen nervously held the bottle, desperately trying to stifle the involuntary shaking of her hand. Would Ellen suspect anything was amiss? Would she question why Helen had agreed after fighting it for some time? Or would her desperation override all?

"Oh, Helen," she said. "I'm so happy that you would do this for me!"

The bottle quit shaking, and Helen smiled.

*Was it finally happening?* Helen and Ellen had sought many opinions over the years, anxious to solve their dilemma. In each case, the doctors had said that the operation would be safe, as far as operations go—safe for Helen. They were very clear on that.

But there were no guarantees for Ellen. The sisters did not share any organs—they were bonded at the hip by flesh and bone, and slightly conjoined at the head. Nonetheless, separation could be fatal for Ellen.

The doctors thought it would work, they liked their chances, but it carried risks.

There was more. Following the surgery, Helen could lead a relatively normal life. But Ellen would almost certainly be wheelchair bound—*if* she survived the separation. There was no getting around it. Her right leg had never fully developed.

So Ellen was unwilling. *Selfish to the core.* And now she wanted her sister to go through the indignity of being present while she made love to her boyfriend. *Disgusting. The nerve!*

The years of bitterness bubbled over. Helen could take no more. The thought drove her. It grew to an obsession. It woke her in the morning and put her to bed at night, where it often kept her awake. Still, as right as it felt, Helen was thorough. She weighed the pros and cons, and recognized the risks. She knew there would be punishment.

The matter was finally resolved when she had a startling revelation. At first, it had made her feel horrible. Ashamed. But no longer. Now, it filled her with a giddy, intoxicating happiness. If Ellen was unable to take a teeny tiny risk so that the two of them could be separated, *then she would be made to separate.* No matter the consequences.

Still, she racked her brain for a clean solution. So many ways the thing could be done, but they were all bloody and gruesome, with lots of screaming. Helen couldn't abide *that.* No, there were better ways. Weren't there?

She felt a wave of relief come over her the day she hit upon just the answer she was looking for. It would be bloody. Oh, yes. But she cared not. She had had enough.

*Let her bleed.*

With the bottle in hand they waddled over to the couch the only way they could, working in perfect harmony. Still, as usual, Helen's back ached from the effort. Together, unified, they sat down.

Ellen was ready. She took a deep breath and determinedly slammed down the dose of sedative. The effect was immediate. Using a mirror she kept handy, Helen watched as her sister's eyelids grew heavy. Soon, they were nearly sealed shut. A strand of drool appeared from a corner of her mouth. She was in between states of consciousness now.

That was Helen's sign.

She poured another dose of the drug, a double dose this time. She stretched her right arm out as far as it could go, reaching over their torso. She held the small medicine cup to her sister's lips.

"Drink this, dear Sister. I measured the dose incorrectly. More is required."

In response, Ellen garbled a bit of incomprehensible gibberish. But she did as she was told and drained the cup, her last conscious action before falling into a deep, unnatural sleep. The poison apple from *Snow White* couldn't have done a better job.

A self-satisfied smile appeared on Helen's face. She breathed deeply, as if lording over her ability to still do so as she watched her sister's chest rise and fall with the last halting breaths of her pathetic life. The sedative worked swiftly; she seemed to grow weaker by the second.

It was peaceful to watch. Liberating. A burden was being removed from her; already, she could feel it.

Helen observed silently for some time before becoming concerned. She tried to brush off her fears, but the effort was futile. Her sister was breathing, as regular as ever. The sedative should be poisoning her by now. Killing her.

Her plan wasn't working. Her sister should be dead!

Panic came over her. How could her sister survive? A titanic dose of a powerful sedative in her little body! It made no sense. Why didn't she do more research? Who was she to think she could kill someone so easily?

*Fine.* She would do the job with Ellen alive. So be it.

Helen forced their shared body to rise from the couch. It was difficult with Ellen unconscious, more so than Helen had expected without their bodies working in harmony. She moved awkwardly, whipping her sister's body around as she did. They went through a doorway, where Ellen's head bounced off the wood. Helen held her breath, but Ellen didn't wake. The sedative was at least strong enough for that. *Thank goodness.*

Helen walked to the garage, struggling to make it to their father's old toolbox. He had died some years ago, leaving behind many tools, and she was reasonably certain that she would find what was needed.

She dug through the toolbox, bright and red, until the cold steel of a hacksaw filled her hand.

Helen had long ago committed the surgery charts to memory. She had requested and received them back when the discussions had taken place, a part of her plan to bring her sister on board. Together, they could discuss the surgery until Ellen grew comfortable with it. But it didn't work, and Ellen would not discuss it. Case closed.

Yet that didn't stop Helen from studying them until she knew exactly where the cuts would have to be made. It was only recently that it had occurred that she herself could make the cuts.

She would begin with the connection at their heads. It was very narrow, directly above their respective ears. She gingerly put the blade to flesh and began to saw, gradually growing more comfortable with the process.

Helen was stunned to find there was no pain. She began to wonder if she was even making a cut. Her answer arrived when warm blood spilled on to her hand.

She finished the cut—the last bit of flesh, rubbery, took some doing as it hung on stubbornly. Helen felt her breaths become short as she pulled her head to the right, slowly severing the bond from her sister. It was an amazing sensation, one that left her mouth open wide. *Ecstasy.*

Helen then saw a side of her sister she had never seen, though the view was obstructed; it was difficult to see through the blood that drenched her face and stung her eyes. Helen stifled a joyous laugh; her stupid sister slept, unaware of the change taking place.

However, Helen's work was far from done. Their hips remained. This would be much tougher. It would hurt, of this Helen was certain. But there was no sense in waiting.

She grit her teeth and began to cut. The pain was agonizing, but there was the satisfaction of seeing more of their shared flesh pulled free.

When the saw met bone, the pain moved a level beyond agonizing. Excruciating didn't quite cover it. Helen resisted the urge to scream, biting down hard on her bottom lip until it too began to bleed.

She took a deep breath, choking back the vomit that wanted to spew forth from the pain. Her eyes drifted to the bottle of sedative. She greedily took it, hoping it would dull the hurt. She twisted free the top to drink directly from the bottle, stopping when she judged she had had enough.

She gave the drug a moment to kick in, and began to cut again.

The saw cut halfway through the bone when it snapped, no longer able to bear their shared weight. Their lifelong bond was broken as her sister involuntarily pulled free. The suffering ran so deep that Helen could no longer stifle her screams. They echoed from the walls, escaping the house and stretching to the open windows of their neighbors. Together, one last time together, they fell to the floor.

Helen hit hard, seeing stars as her head bounced off the laminate floor. Ellen remained unconscious, unmoving and silent. Dead? Perhaps. It mattered not. She was no longer Helen's concern.

Through groggy eyes, Helen shed tears of joy. For the first time, the sisters existed as separate entities. As Helen went unconscious, her last thoughts were on the joy of her success, which stifled the throbbing in her skull.

*** 

In certain observers, the sight of a bride coming down the aisle is guaranteed to bring about tears. These are people who come prepared, stuffing their purses with Kleenex or jamming toilet paper into their pockets for the big moment.

On this day, however, many of the guests were unprepared for the emotions that would beset them. Yes, they knew the couple. They knew her story. But they were unaware that for month upon agonizing month, the bride had practiced with a prosthetic leg. It had been fashioned by a creative, industrious soul, someone who would not take no for an answer. She swore that Ellen would walk someday.

That day was today. When Ellen came down the aisle, walking slowly but assuredly, wearing a broad smile for the husband that awaited, all assembled were left in tears. It was an amazing moment for one who had overcome so much.

All assembled, save one. Tucked in a rear corner of the chapel sat a woman who bore a strong resemblance to the beaming bride. This guest did not beam nor choke back tears. Her face was blank. Emotionless. Cold. Dead. The way it had been since the "accident." *Accident.* There was no better way to describe the events a judge ruled had been caused by insanity. Why she had been invited and why she had shown up was something only the sisters could know.

Despite being let off by the law of the land, the consequences had been severe. She was declared a ward of the state and was little more than a vegetable, surmised by most as being brought on by a combination of head trauma, severe blood loss, and modern psychiatry.

But that face, frozen forever it had seemed, finally cracked. When the groom met the bride at the altar, his gentle grasp wrapping around her waist to support her as they were joined together, the unmoving face in the corner was marked with a solitary tear.

# UPON THE HOUSETOP

A rusting station wagon drove up to a large tan home, brakes whining as it came to a stop. The engine idled roughly, burping white clouds of exhaust. A boy—twenty-two, but he was a boy and would remain so in perpetuity—had been waiting for the wagon impatiently from a big picture window. He disappeared from view and reappeared at the front door. He bounded from the home, shoe laces untied and flopping as he rushed to the car.

He slammed the door behind him, crossed his arms, and grunted as he climbed into the passenger seat. "Ugh!"

His mother sighed. He had been doing so much better with the temper tantrums, but she feared he was gearing up for a big one. Maybe it was time to put an end to these play dates. She knew she was supposed to ignore his fits, but . . .

"What's wrong, Christopher?"

"Ugh! It's not fair!" He kicked at the frayed floor mat, bumping his knee against the glove box as he did, which infuriated him more.

"What's not fair?"

He turned to look at her, though he could not hold eye contact. His face was red, eyes watery. "Santa Claus isn't fair! Paul already has a bunch of stuff, and his parents buy him everything! But Santa already brought him a bunch of presents and they're already under his tree and it's not even Christmas yet! Ugh!"

Her support group was right. It was time for the truth. Past it, in fact. Christopher was 22, Down Syndrome or not, and so what if Paul's mom didn't agree? She could raise Paul how she wanted; Christopher was hers.

The station wagon rumbled off and she took a deep breath. She spun the volume dial on the radio to the left, muting the sound. "Christopher, this is going to be hard for you to hear. It might make you sad."

Christopher slumped in his seat and re-crossed his arms while she gently tried to explain.

*** 

Christopher didn't believe her. He was old enough to know better. Yes, he knew mall Santas were only helpers. After all, some of them didn't even have real beards. Santa couldn't be everywhere. Of course. But he existed. He knew that. There was a Santa Claus.

And Santa was a jerk.

Christopher saw it on TV all the time. Santa picked on poor Rudolph. He kicked Ralphie down the slide. Now, in real life, he gave Paul presents when he already had everything. Christopher would get no presents when he had been good all year long. It wasn't fair that Santa ignored him when mom was out of work and the family needed help more than ever.

He didn't know why, but his mom was lying to protect Santa. Christopher didn't want to hear it. If Santa wanted to spoil the rich kids, like Paul, that was up to him. But Christopher didn't have to take it. In fact, he was going to do something about it.

Christmas Eve couldn't come soon enough.

There was a family with young kids next door—two boys. Christopher sometimes played with them. They were good boys no matter how many times Santa checked his list, so he knew Santa would bring them presents.

But what Santa didn't know was that he would be waiting. He had come up with a plan, a good one, and Christopher was proud of it.

\*\*\*

Christmas Eve was here. Christopher spent the day staring out the side window that faced the neighbor's house. His mother could only watch him and sigh. It was clear that Christopher was depressed about things this holiday even though she had managed to get presents for him after all—but her name was on the gift tags.

Christopher wanted presents from Santa.

He watched as the boys left with their mother. Shortly thereafter, the boy's father came from the garage with a lengthy metal ladder in hand. He disappeared from sight as he took it around back. Soon, he reemerged and returned to the garage, exiting moments later with two large bags from Target. These also went to the backyard. Sometime later, he returned unwinding an extension cord behind him, which he plugged into an outside outlet.

That evening, the boys returned and Christopher heard exclamations of delight as they pointed at the roof. Their dad joined them, looking pleased.

Eventually, the happy family went inside. Meanwhile, his mother had fallen asleep on the couch while *It's a Wonderful Life* played on television. Soon, the lights went out next door and the house was dark.

It was time. Christopher left his window, taking care so that the door did not slam behind him. He trudged through snow and pulled himself over the backyard fence. He watched the house carefully; it was asleep. He crept through the backyard toward it.

He had planned on sneaking into the house, but when he got there, he realized he didn't know how. Besides that, he had the sudden inkling that the boys inside would hardly be asleep at all—when he knew Santa was coming, it took him forever to fall asleep. What was he to do?

*The ladder.* It was still there, propped against the house. Christopher had an idea. Why break into the house, when someone might hear him? No, that was no good—what he would do is wait for jolly old Saint Nick where he would not expect to be bothered—up on the housetop.

The ladder was steel, and cold. His legs wobbled beneath him as he rose rung by rung. Finally, after an awkward struggle, he was over the gutters, feeling rough, cold shingles on his fingers. His feet clicked on the icy slabs as he moved toward the brick chimney, which stood parallel to the peak of the house.

From inside the house two boys, wide awake, had the same thought.

"Do you hear that?" the older brother said.

"Santa!" said the younger.

Christopher made it to the chimney. From there, he could see to the other side of the roof. And Christopher couldn't believe it.

Santa was here, already, and with his reindeer. They had a strange glow about them—a magical glow. Rudolph's nose blinked slowly. There was a slight buzzing sound that came from them—the magic working? Santa was smaller than Christopher expected, but it explained how he could slide down tight spaces.

Christopher wasn't waiting any more. He scrambled over the peak and began to descend.

"I hear the reindeer!" said the older brother.

"They're stomping their hooves!" said the younger.

Christopher felt his feet go out from under him only steps from Santa. The roof was slick; he hadn't been ready for it. As he fell, he shifted his body and lunged for the overwrought elf.

Christopher had him! He wrapped his arms around the belly that shook like a bowlful of jelly. But try as he might, he continued to skate down the sloped roof. Together, entwined, they slid. A cord, protruding from Santa's feet, tugged on a reindeer from the roof, followed by another, and another—nine in all. Bells that were fastened to their necks jingled in the winter air. An extension cord ripped free from the outlet.

Two boys squealed in delight as sleigh bells rang.

Christopher and Santa landed on the driveway. The reindeer followed, piling on top of them.

Santa was dented, a big dip in his stomach. He wore a crack that stretched across his face. Christopher lay upon him, unmoving, covered in plastic figures.

The reindeer were undamaged.

The driveway was streaked in red, which ran down the gentle incline and pooled at the bottom.

A woman looked out of her window. Her tired eyes struggled to see in the dark, but she could clearly make out a collection of plastic reindeer in a pile on their driveway.

"I thought you said you put the decorations up good this year?" she said.

"I thought I did," said her husband, joining her at the window to gaze sadly at the remains of an afternoon's work.

# A RIDE

"Do you mind if I smoke?"

"Yeah, I'm sorry but I do mind."

"That sucks. Do you mind if I ask why? I'll crack the window."

"I don't care for smoke. Cracking a window won't help, it'll still smell. Plus, I just bought this car."

"You just bought *this*?"

"Yeah."

"It's a piece of shit!"

"Yeah, I know it's a piece of shit, but I just bought it."

"Why would you buy this?"

"It's all I could afford. Look, it might be a piece of shit, but it runs. As far as I'm concerned it's a BMW."

"You need to aim higher. That's your problem. You settle. I can see that about you. A BMW is no big deal. I see them all over the place. Every piece of crap real estate agent has one. My folks drive Beemers. Why not say that this a Ferrari to you? Aim higher."

"Whatever, man, you still can't smoke in here."

"So what do you do for a living? Oh, take a right here at the stoplight."

"I know the way. Basically, I do odd jobs and stuff, whatever comes along. How about you? You live in a nice area. How'd you ever afford a house in Ponca Hills?"

"I don't. My parents do. I'm staying there for a bit, until I get back on my feet."

"That sucks, man."

"It's all right, but it'd be nice if they would stop hassling me about everything. They really wanted me out by the end of last year so it's been a little rough—they wouldn't get off my back about it. I'm just waiting for the right job. See, I *don't* settle."

"I see. But I can understand, too—maybe they're ready to be empty-nesters, you know? Raising children wears you out. We all need a break eventually. I've got a couple myself."

"Yeah, I hear you, but you're starting to sound like them—*move out or else*! Jesus, I'm working on it! *Ugh*. Now I have to put the cigarette back in the pack. You ever try to shove a cigarette back in a full pack?"

"No, I haven't. As you may have inferred, I don't smoke."

"It's going to be all bent and stuff. Can't I just smoke this one? One won't hurt."

"One *will* hurt. Cigarette smell lingers. Even one cigarette lingers."

"God damn it. Everyone's against smokers. I'm sick of it!"

"I'm not against smokers, people can do what they want as far as I'm concerned. But I don't like smoke, and I especially don't like smoke in my car. Besides, I don't think people are against *smokers*. We just don't want to breathe in that second-hand stuff."

"People *are* against smokers. Look at the government! They're doing whatever they can to stop people from smoking! Like it's some kind of disease or something."

"I have to call bullshit, man. The government doesn't want you to stop smoking."

"What are you talking about? Every time I turn around they raise the tax on these things."

"Exactly. The government doesn't want you to quit smoking. But you are on to something. What the government *does* want is for the 80% of us who don't smoke to hate those who do. That way we don't feel bad that they're taxing the shit out of you. They demonize smoking, then tax it, and everyone is happy. Except the smokers."

"Where'd you hear that? Did you come up with that?"

"It's just common sense. Think about it. The last thing they want is for you to quit smoking. It's the one thing they can tax without anybody saying anything. And if someone like you does bitch about it, the rest of us just say *if you don't like it, quit smoking.* You see?"

"But they pay for all those anti-smoking commercials on TV. Those ads with the guy with the hole in his throat and so forth, or the kids rapping about cigarettes being lame."

"Have you ever watched those commercials? They show a bunch of dorks talking about how uncool smoking is. They might as well be saying *smoking is cool, don't be like these geeks.*"

"So you're saying they want people to smoke?"

"If they don't, they're doing a hell of a job trying to get people to."

"Well, if it's all about taxes then why don't they legalize weed? And tax the hell out of it like cigarettes?"

"Now you're getting into a whole other area. The pharmaceutical companies and the companies that make the bars for jail cells and so forth are all involved in that one."

"You really think they have that kind of power?"

"Of course they do. They've got money; you don't need anything else. I saw this thing on TV where they were talking about how better off we'd

be if we switched to those little gold dollars instead of paper. It'd save like a billion dollars a year. Some crazy amount, because the coins last longer. But they can't change."

"Why?"

"The cotton industry. A dollar bill is like 75% cotton. We call it paper money, but it's really made of all sorts of materials. So you've got the cotton industry involved, ink companies, all kinds of stuff. It's all screwed up."

"You're stressing me out. You know what I like to do when I'm stressed out?"

"What's that?"

"I like to smoke a cigarette."

"Sorry, man, I'd love to help you."

"No, you wouldn't. If you'd love to help me, you'd let me smoke."

"All right. I'd love to help you, *but* I have certain boundaries that I refuse to cross, and one of those boundaries is that I don't let people smoke in my car. If I had known you were a smoker I would have told you to light one up before we left. But I didn't know. I'm sorry."

"Yeah, me too."

"But let me ask you this—you've got a fresh pack of smokes there. Marlboros, too. How is it that you had money for that but not money for a cab? It's kind of risky accepting a ride from a stranger, no?"

"I suppose so, but you seem all right. I wouldn't get in the car with just anyone, you know?"

"Good thinking."

"Besides, it's not like I *knew* my car wasn't going to start. I'd probably have to wait forever for a cab, too, but you were right there. I figured it wouldn't hurt to ask. Look, I'll give you some gas money—I do appreciate the ride."

"Don't worry about it. But, you know, you could've walked. A walk would've done you some good. It's not that far."

"Hey, I told you that I really appreciate what you're doing. But Jesus, that would be some walk, especially this time of night! If I'm any trouble, I'll be happy to get out and walk the rest of the way—I was very polite when I asked back at the bar, and only said if it was on your way."

"That's true. I'm sorry. You mind if I turn this song up?"

"Naw, go ahead. You like Rage Against the Machine?"

"Yeah, I do, although it never sat well with me that they were so anti-establishment yet they had no problem making millions from their huge record company conglomerate, you know? But I still like them. How about you?"

"Too political for me, man. I want sex and drugs with my rock and roll!"

"Right on. Well, to each their own."

"Hey, what was that? Did you hit a pothole or something?"

"No."

"You sure? I felt something, like my seat sort of moved. Maybe I drank too much."

"It happens."

"Oh, hey, watch out—don't turn here, you're going the wrong way. This road leads into Hummel Park! Better turn around; there's a curfew there. Plus, it's creepy. I hate this place. You can let me out if you want. I can walk home. It's not that far, now. I appreciate the ride."

"Here, I'll turn around—I was just distracted and went the wrong way. I'm sorry, I don't know what I was thinking. Let me turn around. I lost track of what was going on when you started talking about potholes—"

"I felt it again! Is there something in your backseat?"

"Not that I recall. Do you see anything back there?"

"Let me look. Can you turn on your interior light? This is weird."

"All right, hold on. Let me turn the car around first. I need to focus. This road is pretty narrow."

"Dude, something is *totally* back there. I just felt it again. Let me take a look!"

"Hey Bill, quit screwing around and take care of this!"

"Bill? Who the hell is Bill? My name isn't Bill. I told you, it's Jeff."

"I'm not talking to you, pal. Did I forget to introduce you? I guess I spaced it. See, my friend Bill is back there, riding along under a blanket. He's kind of shy, you know? Doesn't like to meet people he's going to, well, strangle."

"Oh my God! Oh my God! What are you doing? Help! Help! Hel—"

"Nice work, Bill—he never knew what hit him. Should've moved out when his parents told him to. See, you better find an apartment, Bill, or you might be next! Ha ha. But God damn, what were you doing back there, bumping into his seat and whatnot? You've got to sneak up better than that. All right, let me turn the car around, and we'll go dump him in that hole you dug and get out of here."

# BODY OF SCIENCE

Landon was the kind of guy that made the coffee at the office. He always arrived well before his co-workers, those sad sacks to whom the coffee appeared as if by magic. They'd roll in ten minutes late, hit the time clock, and head off to fill their mugs, chatting about last night's baseball game without doing a shred of work until they had wasted a good chunk of the day. *Pathetic.* Sure, Landon loved baseball, too, but when there was work to be done, he did it, except for, well, when things spiraled out of control. Then, he just quit showing up for work, period.

But that was long ago. Ancient history. He had been clean since he got out, and he would stay that way. He had no choice, because he wasn't going back. Ever.

So it was with some surprise that when he showed up early to earn a paycheck of sorts, he was not the first one present. Not even close. Here he was, twenty minutes early, yet he was already fifteen back in line. Fifteen!

Who knew that people donating plasma were capable of such over-achievement?

Being so far back put him behind a bunch of scumbags, drug addicts, and alcoholics. In other words, people just like him, or the old him. He had changed, but these people, never. For them, change was an impossibility.

Still, he was here with them. He sighed, thinking over how he'd sunk so low. It wasn't right. He could be doing real work, making real money, but real work and money were hard to come by. All he needed was a break.

Until that break came his way, he'd have to eke by. The word was that donating plasma was worth $50 a week. Stocking shelves part-time at the Dollar Tree wasn't enough, so the money would come handy.

Landon waited in silence, ignoring the banal conversations in front of him while taking occasional glances at his watch. There was no cell phone to occupy his attention; instead, he studied the surrounding shopping center and its large parking lot in great detail. It had been recently updated, with new paint, signage, and asphalt, but it remained the same old supermarket, hardware store, fast food restaurants, and cell phone store you'd find at any other center around town. As he scanned the lot, watching the arriving employees of the scattered businesses spill out of their cars, he made eye contact with a young man holding a clipboard strolling beside a row of cars. The man had semi-long, straw-colored hair that crawled out from underneath a beat-up trucker hat. *A hipster.* Having locked eyes, the man beamed. Seeing his chance, he strode toward Landon.

"What's up, man?" the hipster greeted, his right hand outstretched, which Landon ignored. "You donating today?"

Landon could feel the shame rising in his face. "Yeah," he mumbled. Why did people do this, bothering people who had no interest in being bothered?

"Cool, man. Right on," the hipster said. "You gotta do what you gotta do, right? Plus, you're *helping* people. Always a good thing."

"Yeah," Landon replied. He began to nervously play with his belt buckle, the way he always did when he felt awkward. It was all he had left of his old man, a gaudy cowboy belt, thick leather adorned with stamps of cattle skulls and cacti. "Something like that."

"Well, check it man. I've got something a lot better than donating plasma, and it helps people, too, if you're interested. You got a few seconds?"

Landon cringed. Of course he wasn't interested, but he was fifteen deep in a plasma line. He had a few seconds. He had *many* few seconds.

"Yeah, you could say I've got a few seconds," Landon said dryly.

The hipster laughed, way too enthusiastically. Landon was starting to guess at his angle—Amway salesman? He had heard the pitch many times—*work from your home, a couple of hours a week, cut out the middleman, it happened to me so it can happen to you.* Same old, same old.

"Yeah, bro, I can see that!" the man said while Landon winced. Landon hated being called *bro*. But the hipster took no notice and continued. "Look man, my name is Steve."

"Name's Landon." His old counselor had always said he needed to be more welcoming to people—'don't be so standoff-ish' was her advice, as he recalled. He stuck out his hand, which Steve shook. His grip was strong, his hands rough, not quite fitting the *surfer in the middle of the Midwest* vibe he was trying to present. Landon noticed the hipster's knuckles were scuffed and one of his fingers swollen. Landon once had similar injuries himself; they had come from punching another man in the face. Repeatedly.

"Landon, good to meet you, bro. Listen, I know you're busy but I kind of wanted to talk to you about something. See, I'm with this company–"

Landon cut him off. "Amway, right? I've heard the pitch. It's not for me. But thanks."

"No. *No*, bro, nothing like that! Just give me a second, just a few seconds and listen to me. Times are tough right now, I get it. I know! But listen. I have a way for you to make the easiest $5000 you'll ever see. One hour, boom, five grand. You interested?"

Landon smirked. "Well, of course that would interest me. But really? Nothing is ever that easy. No thanks. Appreciate it." His counselor could say what she wanted; he had been nice enough to the surfer *dude* but that didn't mean he had to stand here and be conned.

Landon turned and took a few steps. The door to the center was finally open and people were starting to trickle inside, moving the line forward.

"So what do they pay you for this? Fifty bucks a week, right?" Steve asked, not discouraged by Landon's first refusal.

"Yeah," Landon said, then smiled. "Plus I heard they give you snacks after, so you don't feel light-headed. I hope they have Nutter Butters. I love those things." Damn that counselor; he just couldn't be outright rude to this kid. Granted, he was a kid that was taller than Landon, wiry with traces of a muscular physique under his Billabong t-shirt.

Steve laughed, again a shade too overeager. "Yeah dude, Nutter Butters! I like those too. Now Landon, look, man, I know it sounds too good to be true. I know! But I'll make it real simple. You sign a paper, we give you five grand, and when you die—we all do, some day!—then the company I represent gets your body for science. It's that simple! No different than what you're doing now by donating plasma, except we don't get anything until you're gone. You won't even have to wait in line."

"I don't know . . ." Landon stammered, wishing the man would leave.

Steve held his hands up in mock surrender and handed Landon his card. "I understand. It's a big decision. Think about it, bro?"

Landon nodded, moving forward in line. "All right. I'll give it a thought."

"Cool bro! You know where to find me. Have a good day!"

Landon moved forward, finally reaching the door while Steve moved on to other targets in the parking lot. Before he entered the plasma center, he looked back for the hipster, but he had disappeared amongst a sea of SUVs and mini-vans.

***

Landon ran his fingers across a bandage on his arm, wincing at the wound that was throbbing slightly. He was sipping on a small carton of orange juice and munching on the last of his Nutter Butters while he waited for his check. When the secretary was occupied, he discretely snatched another bag and stuffed it into his pocket.

He was growing restless. The lobby television was tuned to a cable news network, with a talking head going on and on about drug testing Welfare recipients—as if drug addiction was simply a switch one could turn on or off. *If only.*

He wondered if the men that surrounded him wished it was so. Perhaps not; a lot of the addicts he knew seemed to enjoy being miserable. Landon studied his fellow donors and grimaced. They were clad in tattered shoes and clothing, all of them, and were stuffing bags of snacks into their pockets the same way he had. Someone in the group smelled strongly of body odor. In fact, the whole place stunk.

How had he sunk so low? This was no place for him. He had tried it and it wasn't for him. He didn't belong here, and he didn't want to come back.

Landon turned his attention back to the television when the talking head said something that registered. *"The body of science tells us . . ."*

Perhaps he didn't have to return here. What could it hurt to give this Steve a call? Maybe he wasn't full of it. Landon was already at rock bottom—he was staring at it all around him, hearing it, smelling it.

The secretary called him up to the counter. He collected his check and nodded at the woman as she explained where he could cash it. He thanked her, finished the last sips of the juice, threw the container into the trash, and left the center behind. He hoped to never return.

Landon knew what he had to do, now. It was worth a shot. He would look for Steve outside. Failing that, he would find a pay phone, assuming there were any around, and make the call.

Maybe it was all a scam. Maybe it was too good to be true. But if it was legit, well, it could change everything. If it wasn't, well, what was the worst that could happen? Besides, what was he going to do with his body when he was dead?

For once, he couldn't lose.

***

A gray-haired woman wearing a lab-coat walked up to Landon and handed him a clipboard.

"Good afternoon, Mr. Douglas," she began. "Thank you for choosing to work with MLM Industries today. First, I want to be clear about what is taking place. We are only paying you for the successful completion of this survey. Any donation of your body in the name of science is a charitable gift from you and no monetary compensation is provided nor implied for such a promise."

"I understand," Landon said.

"Good," she said. She handed him a pen. "Just sign on the line and that will take care of that."

Landon briefly scanned the document. It appeared to be in order, containing the same legalese that documents of this type always seemed to have. Good enough for him.

Landon signed.

"Now the process is quite simple. You have signed paperwork making MLM the recipient of your body upon death. Again, this is only a donation. Now you must complete a 100-question survey as part of our study in order to be paid. The questions are quite simple. Please answer them as honestly as possible so that the maximum benefit can be gleaned from your donation. When you are finished, please leave the survey with me, at which time you will be given your check. Do you have any questions?"

Landon shook his head. "No, I think it is all quite clear."

"Good!" She handed over a freshly sharpened number-two pencil. He sat down and looked over the survey, which was covered with bubble spaces for him to mark his answers. Landon felt like he was back in high school, taking the ACT.

Some good that 32 score ended up doing him.

*Name?* Easy enough. *Height, weight, date of birth, social security number?* Nothing he couldn't handle. *Address?* Had to think for a moment. There hadn't been many reasons to use the address of the home where he rented an old lady's basement apartment. Generally, the less people that knew where he lived, the better.

The questions picked up a bit in the next section. *Marital status?* Divorced. *Glasses/contacts?* No. *Allergic reactions?* None. Well, alcohol didn't seem too react too well with him, but that was something else entirely. *Seizures/Epilepsy?* No. *Concussions? Hmm.* That made him think. There had been a few, years ago, back in high school football. Yes. *Stroke?* No. *High cholesterol?* No clue. Hadn't seen a doctor in years.

He filled in "No."

The questions went on from there—they seemed especially interested in his concussions—but after a half-hour or so, he was finished. He fastened the pencil to the clipboard and returned to the counter, which was separated from the lobby by a glass partition. He could see the gray-haired woman with her back turned, working over a copy machine. He waited for some time, not wishing to hit the little bell on the counter to get her attention. She'd see him soon enough.

One minute turned to two and two turned to three—how many copies was she making? As the time dragged on, he looked around the office, smirking as he thought about the disparity between the clean and tidy office he was in now and the disheveled Steve that had recruited him. Finally, after waiting five minutes he took action, coughing softly at first, then a bit more loudly when she didn't notice. Finally she turned, saw Landon, and strode to the counter.

She pulled back the glass partition and took the clipboard as it was handed to her, flipping through the pages briefly to ensure all of the questions were completed.

"Thank you very much, Mr. Douglas," she said. "This all seems to be in order." She reached down to her desk and lifted an envelope with his name typed across the front. She handed it to Landon, who accepted eagerly.

"Thank you," he said. He opened the envelope and confirmed the amount on the check was correct, then paused. There was something he had not considered.

"Do you know where I can cash this? I seem to be, um, between bank accounts, at the moment."

"Certainly," the woman said. "City Bank and Trust. Their only branch is located on 19th and Farnam. They are used to getting checks from us. Just go there, show them your ID, they'll get your fingerprint, and then you will receive your funds. But do be careful, Mr. Douglas. That bank is not in the best part of town. I'd secure your funds as soon as possible."

Landon nodded, staring at the dollar amount and feeling joy wash over him. *Five-thousand dollars.* "Thank you. Thank you very much."

"Have a good day, Mr. Douglas."

\*\*\*

Friday. *Payday.* The bank was jammed full when Landon finally finished his mile-long walk from the bus stop to the branch office. He fell in at the end of the line, keeping his hand in his pocket so as not to lose his check. He was lost in his thoughts, seeing everything and noticing nothing, when his eyes finally settled on a man walking to a teller station.

It was Steve, the hipster recruiter. He held a wad of bills, which he slapped on the counter. Landon watched as the teller counted the money, forming small piles as she reached certain points during her count. When she finished, there were several stacks of bills piled wantonly. *Those guys must make some serious dough off of this.*

The teller finished counting and began processing the transaction. Landon had no desire to be seen by Steve nor be called *bro* or *dude*, so he removed a safe deposit box brochure from a display and pretended to study it intently. Shortly thereafter, Steve walked by, never slowing his stride nor taking notice.

Landon let out a sigh of relief.

After some time, the teller that had waited on Steve waved him to her window. Landon could feel his palms sweat as he approached, worried that the entire thing would collapse here at the brink of success.

"Good afternoon, sir," the teller greeted. She was a young girl who looked like she had enjoyed many sessions at the tanning booth. She was pretty, but in a way that wouldn't hold up as she aged if she stayed on that path. Already, her skin had a leathery quality.

"Hello," Landon replied. "I need to cash a check. It's off this bank, but I don't have an account here."

The teller took the check and the state ID that he had set on the counter. She looked the items over, then typed the account number into her computer. Her long fingernails glided deftly over the keyboard. He never could understand how women were able to type with those long nails.

"I just need you to endorse the back of the check and then put your right-hand index print on the front with the inkpad on the counter."

Landon held up his index finger. "This one?"

"Yes, sir."

He pressed down on the pad and paused with his finger hovering over the check. "Where should I stamp it?"

"Anywhere you can find room, sir."

Landon did as instructed, finding a blank space above the dollar amount. The ink felt greasy on his finger.

"If you just rub your fingers together, the ink should rub off," the teller said.

"Thanks, Susan," Landon said, reading her name tag. She smiled in a way that made Landon know that she did not particularly enjoy having strangers say her name. He wouldn't use it again.

Landon could feel his heart beat in his ears as she examined the check, holding it up to compare it to something on her computer screen. He couldn't shake the feeling that he was doing something wrong, though he didn't know exactly what that could be. What could be wrong about it?

Just as he started to think of ways to escape, the teller slid the check into some kind of machine. A mechanical printing sound whirred through the lobby and the teller reached into her drawer.

"It's a good thing someone just gave me a bunch of large bills," she said. "Are hundreds all right, Mr. Douglas?"

"Sure," Landon said. It was working! And why shouldn't it? "Hundreds would be great." Then he thought of something. "If you could break the last one into smaller change, I'd appreciate it."

"Certainly," she said.

\*\*\*

Five-thousand dollars in his pocket and not a single thing to buy. He'd gone without for so long that his imagination for copious consumption was almost totally gone. He treated himself to a double Whopper—he'd always wanted to try one—but once that was devoured, the urge to spend more was sated. He shuddered when he thought of what he would have once done with this kind of dough. He shuddered again when the advice of the gray-haired woman spun through his head: "That bank is not in the best part of town." The money in his pocket suddenly seemed a terrible burden, one he must be relieved of. His fingers clutched the currency envelope mashed in his jeans pocket and he watched all passersby as if they were the devil themselves. He couldn't take being out here, alone and exposed, any longer.

It was time to catch the bus and head home to watch some baseball.

\*\*\*

Landon stepped through his apartment door, relieved, and quickly shut it behind him. For the first time, he set the chain lock along with the dead bolt. He walked over to the windows, ensuring they were locked as well.

It had been some time since he had owned anything worth protecting. Nobody would have bothered about the meager possessions in his apartment before, but things had changed.

Still, he was home, and Landon felt himself relax, especially when he turned his attention to other matters—namely, baseball. One of the nice things about living in someone's basement was that he was able to tap into their cable feed. He kicked back in a La-Z-Boy recliner rescued from the curbside trash—it leaned to the left, smelled of wet dog when the weather was humid, and made a grinding noise when he rocked, but other than that it was perfectly fine. He found a Mets-Padres game, staying tuned as it went into extra innings. He didn't care for either team, but baseball was baseball, and who could turn off a tie game?

The Padres walked off with a victory after a wild pitch brought home a run in the bottom of the 15th while Landon dozed off in his chair.

***

The first thing he noticed when he woke up was that he had forgotten to brush his teeth before he fell asleep. He hated when he did that; he had done it far too many times after sleeping a load off.

The second thing he noticed was that somebody was in his apartment with him. A man, hidden in shadow. Landon scrambled out of his recliner; the rickety chair toppled over and fell to the floor, bringing him down with it. He stumbled to his feet and tried to call out for help, but before he could do so the man was on him, wrapping the crook of his arm over Landon's mouth. His other arm held a gun, which he pressed against Landon's waist, near his belt buckle.

"Shh," the man said. Landon was terrified. What could this man want with him?

Then he remembered the money, still wadded up in the envelope in his pocket.

"Remember me, bro?"

Landon grimaced. He should have known. The arm slackened slightly over his mouth. "How'd you get in here?" Landon asked as the grip again tightened.

"Shh," the man said. "I've been waiting for you. You should lock your windows when you're not home, *bro*." It was Steve. *Of course.* He was here for the money. *Too good to be true.*

It was a scam after all, though Landon was having trouble putting the pieces together. Was Steve in business for himself or did MLM Industries have something to do with this? He couldn't puzzle it out, giving up when he realized it didn't matter.

Landon reached into his pocket for the money. He was over it. It was only money; there was no need to get himself killed. Life would go on as it always did. He was already forgetting it; with a little effort, it would be like the money never existed.

He'd be back in line at the plasma bank on Monday.

"I don't want that, Landon. Well, not yet. No, I'm afraid to say it's *you* that I want. Well, not really *you*. Just your body. But I guess since you're one and the same, you've got to come with. *Bro*." The slow drawl Steve had used earlier was gone. His words had menace, and Landon wanted to be sick. The *surfer hipster dude bro* thing was all an act. But what was he talking about?

"You have it already! I signed the paperwork," Landon gasped. "I did everything you asked. As soon as I'm dead, it's yours."

Steve smiled tightly. "Exactly. You said it. *As soon as you're dead.* One problem. You're still alive."

*This wasn't making any sense.*

Steve continued. "They tell me I shouldn't do it this way. My orders are quite clear: kill them while they sleep. One shot of poison and they'll never know what hit them. But is that *fair*? I did it that way, once. Never again. Who wants their last memory to be a dream? No, everyone deserves one last chance to live."

"Are you crazy?" Landon choked out. "Everyone wants to die in their sleep!"

"Wrong!" Steve yelled out, rather loudly. Landon imagined his landlord hearing the shout, waking, calling the police. Surely they would arrive any moment now. "That's what everyone says, but who wants that? To die and never even know it? To go to bed, another day ahead of you, only to never awaken? Terrible! No way, *bro*. I'm giving you a chance. Make your amends with whatever gods you pray to, say your good-byes, and then . . ."

He didn't need to finish the sentence.

"But why now? What's the hurry? This is insane. Do they need bodies that badly?"

"Well, sort of," Steve said. "It's your brain they want, really. At least that's how it was explained to me. Concussion research is huge right now, bro! But there's only so many brains to go around. NFL players don't off themselves for the cause every day, you know? Lot of big-time quarterbacks missing time because of concussions right now. Lots of research that needs done, but not enough brains to go around. Especially brains of known concussion sufferers."

Landon could feel the sweat dripping down his forehead. He thought back to, well, everything. Countless memories dashed through his head, but they were all fleeting, passing through the way clouds would float by on a windy day. There was nothing to cling to, nothing that warranted slowing down the visions. Chaos, disorder, noise, pain, failure. Little more.

But it wasn't his time. Not yet. There could be more memories. Better memories. He was only 35 for God's sake!

Steve readjusted his grip on Landon, which was the opportunity he was waiting for. With the hold momentarily slackened Landon saw his chance and threw a sharp elbow into Steve's ribs. The grip was broken now; Landon slipped free. He found himself face to face with his assailant and struck Steve's hand, sending the gun to the ground. Raging, Steve grabbed Landon by the shirt, while Landon reached for Steve's legs. They wrestled around, with Landon getting in a good jab to Steve's chin, but he was eventually overpowered by his deceptively strong attacker, who found himself on top of a writhing Landon. He drove his knee down hard, grinding Landon's face into the carpet, then fumbled in his pocket and withdrew a hypodermic needle. Poison. Steve wasn't even sure what it was made from, not that it mattered. It would kill and that was enough.

Steve began to raise the needle toward Landon's side. Landon struggled against his grip, but there was no breaking it. Steve was too strong. The needle drew closer and Landon squirmed. It drew closer until it poked through Landon's shirt, near the hip, the only place Steve could reach while maintaining his hold on his victim. It wouldn't be long now.

Steve drove the needle in. He pushed down and released the liquid, then let Landon go. It was all over now, for the poison worked fast.

Steve rolled on to his back, panting but satisfied. He could see the needle protruding from Landon's side and knew the job was done.

But to Steve's great surprise, Landon rose to his feet. The needle had not pierced flesh; rather, it was jammed in his belt, the thick leather preventing any penetration. Landon pulled the needle free and flung it aside; the poison spilled down his pants, harmless.

Landon sprinted for the door to complete his triumphant escape. He even still had the money! He undid the bolt, then pulled. *Damn it.* The door only cracked a few inches before it came to a jarring stop. *The chain!* The chain that he never used. The stupid chain he had latched only tonight, to prevent any intruders, had stopped the door from opening further.

The one time he used that damn chain . . .

His fingers fumbled as he re-closed the door and slid the chain off. He prepared to open the door and run like hell, but when he reached for the handle, the door swung open. It struck him hard on the crown of his head.

Landon went down in a heap. Steve walked over quietly as a large man came through the apartment door. Backup. Just in case.

This was the first time he was ever needed.

"Looks like there's another concussion for them to study, bro," Steve said. They pulled Landon's unconscious body from the threshold into the apartment. The large man closed the door behind them while Steve dug through Landon's pocket. Finding what he wanted, he stood and withdrew another needle from a small case in his pocket while his cohort unrolled a black body bag. The cohort began to wrap Landon in the bag, the zipper getting stuck on the same belt that only moments earlier had extended Landon's life. While he struggled with that, Steve drove the second needle in.

"Bag him and tag him, bro," Steve said, attempting to lighten the mood while he looked inside the envelope he had taken from Landon's pocket. But his cohort didn't laugh. He was all business as he shoved Landon further in the bag, then ripped a blanket free from the bed. The cohort draped the blanket over the body bag, then lifted the bundle over his shoulder and carried it from the apartment.

"Next time, follow the instructions, Steve," the large man said, struggling under the weight of the body as they went outside. "Just kill them in their sleep, man."

A trunk slammed shut, keys jingled as they were turned in the ignition, and a car accelerated, cutting through the late night quiet as it drove off to MLM Industries.

# THE RECEPTION

The toilet flushed in the stall next to Darryl, followed by the sound of a zipper going up and a belt buckle being fastened. An old man shuffled out the door, not even stopping to rinse off his hands in the sink. Darryl shuddered. The idea! How could someone not wash their hands after doing whatever ungodly thing they had been doing in that stall? It was repulsive.

Still, it was to Darryl's benefit, as it left him alone in the restroom, and he needed to wrap this up. Thumping music echoed loudly off the walls but at the song's conclusion, that'd be it; he hadn't programmed the set any further. He mentally went over what to play next—even without being able to see the dance floor, he'd figure out something. Darryl knew how to keep the party going, unlike the idiot that was propped up on the toilet in front of him. To think if this jackass had gotten his way—it would've been a disaster, all for the amusement of a handful of nitwit kids.

Darryl snickered. *Now, he didn't get his way, did he?*

Without further delay Darryl pulled up his pants, then lifted his leg up to step onto the toilet paper holder, a silver box that was mounted on the stall wall. He peeked over the divider to make certain the way was clear; it was, so he pulled himself to the top of the wall. The smell of the old man lingered, wafting to the ceiling. *My God, what did he do in here?* Darryl dropped down from the divider, giving the toilet a needed courtesy flush as he landed. He left the old man's stall and went to the sink, letting the water run until it was good and hot. He pumped out a handful of liquid soap and washed his hands, taking a last glance back at the other stall to inspect his handiwork. Darryl nodded, satisfied. *Nobody would look twice.* Anyone else would only see a man sitting on the toilet with his pants around his ankles, nothing that didn't happen in a public restroom countless times throughout the day.

Darryl pushed open the door and returned to the dance floor, smiling at the bride as she whirled around in her wheelchair, dancing excitedly with her new husband. He weaved in and out of sweating dancers to return to his setup, remembering on the way that it was time for the mother-son dance—he had nearly forgotten. He made a few remarks, carefully rehearsed, as he replaced the blaring dance song with Boyz II Men's "A Song for Mama."

His very own recommendation.

***

When they had met beforehand to make arrangements—what songs to play, dances to do, and so forth—Darryl liked the couple right off. The two of them had been together for some time and had overcome much to make it to the altar. It was inspiring, really. Yeah, they had requested some songs to play during the reception, but they weren't pushy about it, and gave him room to open it up beyond those chosen few. Darryl came highly recommended and they trusted him. He liked that.

Even better, they had a few requests for songs *not* to play; among these were "The Chicken Dance." Darryl could've kissed them; he had never had this happen before. That God damn "Chicken Dance." There wasn't a wedding he had worked where some kid hadn't asked him to play it. Try as he might to avoid it and push the kid aside, their beleaguered parent would inevitably stumble up to the deejay stand and make the request.

"Listen buddy," they'd say. "My kid wants 'Chicken Dance.' Can you make sure and play it? You do have it, don't you?"

Darryl wished he could've said no. It would've been so easy to not bring it, to say, "You know what, I don't have it." But that would've been a lie, and Darryl didn't like to lie. Too dangerous. You couldn't run from a lie; they'd always catch up. So yeah, he had "Chicken Dance," because most couples weren't like this one—those couples actually requested that he *did* play it, and worse, they wanted him to pair it with "Cotton-Eyed Joe" or "Electric Slide."

"Let the kids have some fun," those couples would say. "They can burn off some steam. It'll be fun."

It was horrible.

And so he did play those songs for the little monstrosities, and yes, it did seem to make them so damned happy—but most of the adults, the ones with any class, they would sit down, and he'd lose them. Poof, they were gone. Party over, turn out the lights. He'd rarely get them back, no matter how hard he worked.

When the party died, Darryl knew that some people in the crowd blamed him. It drove him insane. They would think he was a hack. A joke. It wasn't true, and it made him sick for people to think otherwise. Ate him alive, because Darryl was the best. He knew that. Being a deejay was an *art form*. It took *skill*. Darryl worked hard at his *craft*. Yet that was pushed aside so some idiots could flap their arms around with their elbows out.

The sick freaks.

Look at the wedding he had done at the Omaha Country Club. The mayor's son. There was lots of money in that ballroom. Big players.

Movers and shakers. Opportunities. Darryl could see himself hosting cocktail parties and big events for the elite. This was his chance.

But just when the alcohol started to take effect on some of those rich snobs, loosening them up a bit and driving them to the dance floor, a bunch of their damn kids began with their pestering. They started yelling out that they wanted him to play this, that, and the other thing, and if he had thoughts of doing otherwise, the scowls on the faces of their parents told him he better do what they said, or else.

Once he ran through the unholy trinity, the party was a dud. The big offers never came. All thanks to "Chicken Dance" and its vile brethren.

Darryl didn't think he could take it any longer. They might as well slap him in the face and say, "Look pal, we have no respect for what you do. Anyone can keep the party going. You're nothing but a loser. You've wasted your life. A chimp can do what you do. Now go play 'Chicken Dance,' 'Cotton-Eyed Joe,' 'Electric Slide,' and shut up."

They were destroying him slowly, an infectious wound that was growing more poisonous as each wedding drove the knife deeper.

\*\*\*

This wedding, this wonderful wedding that had begun so beautifully, so perfectly, with the couple treating his expertise with the deference it deserved, was dissolving in front of his eyes. It was terrible to behold. In fact, with such lofty hopes instilled in him, it was shaping up to be the worst one of all.

It began before the bride and groom had even made their entrance. Darryl was approached by a middle-aged man with a receding hairline, glasses, and protruding gut. Before he had said a word Darryl knew what the man would ask. Sure enough, he did. "Can you play that 'Chicken Dance' song? My kids love it."

Darryl felt his body tense. There were countless classic songs that he could play for those kids, songs that wouldn't rot their brains while expanding their musical knowledge. The Beatles. The Beach Boys. The Stones. Motown. Songs made with talent. Art. He didn't need trickery to keep the kids happy. He especially didn't need a suggestion from this clown. He was a professional. A *highly recommended* professional.

Darryl sized the man up, seeing and smelling that he had already taken ample advantage of the open bar, with a half-empty plastic cup in his clutches to prove it. He'd be drunk soon enough, and lucky to remember his children's own names. This conversation would be long forgotten. Darryl shrugged. *Might as well humor him.* No reason not to, especially if it would get this man away from his booth.

"Sure thing. I'll take care of it later tonight, once we get all settled in."

"Thanks man. Say, want me to get you a beer or something?"

Darryl politely declined; he never mixed business with pleasure. He didn't get to be the best by imbibing, then slurring out heartfelt wishes for the newlyweds.

As the night went on, Darryl watched as the man hit the bar again, and again, and again. Darryl had never seen anything like it, yet the man seemed hardly phased. Worse, he wasn't letting it drop; every time he walked by he would flap his arms. What would possess a man to act so?

The pig.

In short order, the man came by again and bellied up to the bar, flapping his arms at Darryl as they made eye contact. He balanced two foamy beers and returned to his table. His children—three of them—were bored, staring at the screens of their phones and yawning. As the man sat down, the bride stopped by, making her rounds, and the drunk proceeded to converse sloppily with her, flapping his arms yet again and pointing toward the deejay station.

Darryl couldn't help but cringe. His ally was lost, he just knew it. The bride was too caught up in the moment. Knee-deep in joy and expensive champagne, "Chicken Dance" didn't seem so bad, not when the faces of the man's children looked so glum.

Darryl knew there was no escape; "Chicken Dance" was inevitable, and "Cotton-Eyed Joe" and "Electric Slide" along with it.

When the bride moved on to another table the man tipped his cup upwards and took a long swig before slamming it on the table, drips of brown suds staining the white tablecloth. He leaned over to his wife, spoke in her ear, and staggered to the restroom. Darryl felt himself shake and his stomach lurch.

This was his chance. He knew what had to be done. He had to make a stand. These people were killing him. *Killing his soul.* What man could abide that? When would he say *enough*?

He quickly queued up the next three songs and made his move. It was the perfect time—the only formality remaining for the evening was the traditional parent dances. Darryl bee-lined after his target, moving so fast that the drunk paused and held the door for him.

"Thanks," Darryl said. Before the man could ask or, God forbid, flap his arms again, Darryl cut him off. "Coming right up," he promised. "After the parent dance, we'll play a few for the kids and get them all tuckered out for you."

"Thanks," the man said, the word slightly drawn out. Beads of sweat were rolling down his forehead. Perhaps the drinking was finally starting to wear him down. The man nodded, then wiped his sweat with his forearm, and went into an open stall.

Darryl watched him and froze. He looked over the facility, getting the lay of the land. The bathroom was crammed, holding two stalls, a sink, and a urinal. His chest thumping, Darryl gathered himself and went over to that lone urinal. They were all alone. This was his chance, and he knew what had to be done. His soul and his pride depended on it. They were begging him to stand up for them just *once*, to put his foot down and draw the line. But when he took a few deep breaths, he knew it was over. He couldn't do it. The man had kids after all. The rage subsided. The moment passed. He had suffered for his art and he would suffer some more, but Darryl felt good; he was doing the right thing. Even better, there was a chance that the man was nearly done for—why, he just might pass out at his table and forget his incessant request.

The two toilets flushed in unison. Darryl went to the sink; meanwhile, the man was having trouble with his door. He fumbled with the lock, confounded. The lock rattled, the struggle violent, the man completely stymied by his inability to open the door. All he had to do was slide a little piece of metal over to unbar it, but the alcohol and his own stupidity wouldn't let him. It was annoying. Pathetic. It was driving Darryl crazy. This man, this insipid man and countless others like him had ruined his life, kept him from being recognized for what he was, which was the *very best*. Darryl exhaled. He was going to stay strong. Let it pass. Move on.

Bury it, he told himself. Don't let him get to you. You're better than this.

The struggle continued. The stall door shook and clanged, as if the issue was with the alignment of the lock and not the user. Finally, there was a pause, and Darryl thought the man had passed out, perhaps, when once again the door jiggled.

Then things took a turn for the worse. Despite his struggles, the man began to hum. Happily, joyfully hum.

And he was humming "Chicken Dance."

Darryl could take no more. If Darryl let him walk, there'd be no escape. Doomed to a life of playing those horrid songs in perpetuity.

He couldn't.

His black dress shoes squeaked on the damp porcelain floor as he streaked to the stall. While he moved, the man finally solved the latch, but it was too late, for when the door began to open, Darryl struck. He reached out and shoved, driving the door swiftly inward. The door thudded as it bounced off the man's skull and threw him to the back of the stall. The ceramic toilet tank lid clinked as the man's torso jarred it loose; only Darryl's swift reflexes prevented it from crashing to the floor.

Darryl kicked the stall door shut behind them while the man struggled to regain his balance. He was nearly steady before Darryl's hands found themselves wrapped around his neck. The man gasped for air, his face changing from cream to bright red to blue. He tried to pry the choking hands away but there was no fight left in him. The drinking and the hard blow from the stall door had left him weak. Soon, he went limp, as limber as a gutted fish, and his shoulders and neck were laid to rest against the toilet tank. Darryl moved swiftly to unzip the man's pants, then pulled

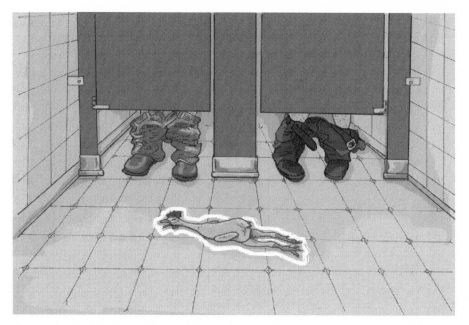

them down to the man's ankles. It was a job well done, and Darryl's soul rejoiced.

But as he turned to leave, the bathroom door swung open. Darryl lifted up his victim's feet and turned so that he faced forward, making sure only his shoes could be seen from below the stall door. His mind racing, he unzipped his pants and let them fall to his ankles to complete the illusion. An old man's shuffling feet passed his stall and shut the door next to his, the latch sliding into place shortly thereafter.

He was trapped, not wishing to draw attention by leaving behind what would show as an occupied stall, and so he was left to hope the old man had taken his Metamucil. Still, Darryl had avoided detection, and he couldn't help but smile at his quick thinking and planning.

\*\*\*

There would be no playing of the "Chicken Dance" nor "Cotton-Eyed

Joe" or the "Electric Slide." Darryl made sure of that as he hastily programmed the rest of the evening's tunes into his player. He went through the introductions of the parents as their respective dances commenced, doing so while risking glances at the confused faces of the man's children as they began to grow more concerned as the minutes passed.

Once the parent dances finished, Darryl excused himself as he hurriedly walked by the beaming married couple, saying he had forgotten something in his van. The bride looked as if she had something to say but his legs never slowed enough to hear it. He left the reception hall, the heavy doors slamming behind him, started his mini-van, and sped off into the night, wondering if he would ever be forced to play "Macarena" in Mexico.

# DEER SEASON

*Daybreak. Devil's Slide. Hummel Park. Omaha, Nebraska. From that bleak hill comes a small pop, followed by a tiny hole appearing in the window of a passing truck. The clear glass turns to spider webs. Tires squeal; the pickup slams to a stop. The door swings open, and the window splinters further into hundreds of tiny squares. A large man, dressed in camouflage and an orange safety vest, stumbles out. The door slams; glass cascades to the concrete like a waterfall. The man dumps his coffee onto the road, along with shards of glass that had fallen into the mug. He holds his hand over his eyes, grimacing as he peers up the hillside where he guesses the shot had come from.*

Devil's Slide was a steep bluff, a cliff nearly, on the eastern edge of the infamous Hummel Park. At its crown it was stripped nearly bare of plants and trees from years of heavy erosion, leaving behind a wide slick of loose topsoil, clumps of brush, and exposed tree roots. Although it was perilous for hiking, that didn't stop many who dared to traverse the precipice to take in the wide vista of the Missouri River valley that spread out in all its glory to the East. Some park visitors would actually attempt to use the slope like a slide for a cheap thrill, while others waited for the sun to go down, when they would come to sip from beers or participate in otherwise dubiously legal activities.

Or, if you were like Preston and Bryce, you came here to shoot at crap with your pellet gun. They had spent the night, camping illegally. The night had been uneventful; so far, the morning had been worse. None of the promised scares that Hummel Park was said to offer had materialized. There had been no hauntings, supernatural events, or unusual noises that couldn't be explained. They had even counted the so-called Morphing Stairs numerous times, but they arrived at the same number each time: 187. Hummel Park had been a total dud.

Sleep had been hard to come by, so they were up early, and bored. If Bryce and Preston wanted excitement, they'd have to create it themselves, seeing as Hummel Park was even less fun with the sun up. All they could think to do was to take their pellet gun and use it to shoot at any old thing—tree trunks, street signs, a fence post. But that too grew boring; the pellets would simply hit their target and bounce off weakly. What else was there? Shooting animals or even birds wasn't their thing, but when a car drove by on the road below, they had their idea.

The drivers took no notice as BBs ricocheted off their cars while they sped down the road; the pellets were as harmless as a piece of gravel as they made tiny pings against plastic and sheet metal. Even this thrill did not last long, so they agreed it was time to retrieve their bicycles from the leaf piles they had buried them in and begin the long pedal home.

Then Preston heard a loud truck roaring toward them. Tantalized, he decided to take one last shot.

What was it about one last anything that always seemed to backfire?

After pulling the trigger, Preston, fifteen and blond, stared at the shattered window from behind a clump of brush that was keeping him hidden. His knees went weak; he wanted to throw up. *What had he done?*

Bryce, his good friend, also fifteen but not blond, stood in disbelief.

"You moron! Why'd you do that?"

Preston gulped. He had never been good at story problems, never could do the math to figure out when two moving cars would meet. "I didn't mean to! Oh, man. I was aiming for the door."

"Well, you missed! Way to go. I warned you! *Don't shoot any windows.* Didn't I?"

The truck door opened and a man staggered out, looking up into the bluff for the shooters. The door slammed closed nearly as fast as it had been opened. The boys looked at each other, speechless, as the truck's engine sprung back to life. They heard the familiar whine of a vehicle going into reverse, then the gears click as it shifted into drive. With a roar, it sped down the road and turned at the first right, zipping by a concrete sign that read *Hummel Park.*

"Shit man, what are we going to do?" Preston blurted.

"Run!" Bryce replied.

"Good idea."

They moved without plan or rationale, allowing their legs to carry them where they wanted. First they scrambled up the Slide, using trees for support where they could find them. They reached flat ground and ran as fast as they could, stupidly leaving the cover provided by the woods for the open park road that cut across the hilltop.

The truck engine screamed as it throttled up the hill, on a path toward them. Unlike his friend, Bryce didn't mind story problems. But this one was demented; it pained him as he figured out that the pickup would be there in only moments.

"Keep running!" he shouted. "Go into those trees!"

They went deeper into the park, tearing past a playground and a picnic shelter as they moved toward a section of dense timber. They came to a worn trail where the grass was flattened, following it until it changed into a smooth, paved surface which wound around and turned until it became a long, uneven, crumbling stairway. They knew it well, for it was the Morphing Stairs. They stepped onto them and began their descent.

Back on the road, the truck screeched to a stop. The cab door slammed, then metal clanged as the pickup's toolbox opened and closed. Hearing this, the boys panicked and left the stairs, veering deeper into the hilly woods to search for a good hiding place. They stumbled through thick clumps of weeds and fallen tree branches, poison nettles stung them, and thick vines reached out and tripped them. Their mad dash ended only when they found themselves in a small ravine, one filled with piles of damp autumn leaves.

"Quick," Bryce ordered, scooping up handfuls of the leaves. "Cover up with these."

Soon, they were completely hidden, with only their eyes visible. After an interminable wait, sweating and panting, Preston could wait no more. He rose from his hiding place to peer out of the ravine and into the greater woods, fervently hoping that the man had given up and left.

But it was not to be. Atop the stairway there stood an overweight black man clad in a bright orange vest with camouflage print underneath. His right hand was wrapped around the stock of a large rifle; his left shielded his eyes as he quietly scanned the woods.

"Oh my God, Bryce," he gasped softly, ducking back down. "He's a hunter, Bryce. He'll hit us if he sees us, for sure," Preston hissed.

"Then don't let him see us," Bryce said. "Just stay put."

Bryce's stomach lurched when he heard the man—*the hunter*—grunt. He must have heard them. Bryce looked at Preston and held his finger to his lips while the hunter's feet scraped against rock as he came down the stairs. The hunter soon came into view and Bryce watched as he would stop every so often to look through the scope and aim the rifle into the woods.

Bryce knew the man wasn't hunting deer. He could hardly believe what one dumb mistake had wrought, and grieved their plight. This man that had gone out on a crisp fall day for deer, or rabbits, or whatever it was that hunters went after was now hunting *them*.

The hunter turned his back to the boys and waved his gun at the other side of the hill. Maybe he hadn't heard them after all. With any luck, he'd soon give up and leave.

Meanwhile, Bryce could hear Preston's breathing grow heavier. He was too panicky, maybe even starting to go into shock. *"Damn it, Preston, calm down,"* Bryce whispered.

But Preston seemed not to hear him. Instead, he rocked on his heels and made a break for it. Without a word he was gone, with leaves crunching under his racing feet, running until he found cover behind a wide, ancient cottonwood tree.

The hunter heard the disturbance and swung back around. He aimed the weapon, located Preston in his sight, and pulled the trigger. The shot banged as Preston reached the tree, arriving only milliseconds before chunks of bark exploded through the air.

Bryce was speechless. On top of everything else, his friend was abandoning him, leaving Bryce to fend for himself against this maniac. Of all the people in Omaha, how was it that they came to break this lunatic's window?

The hunter lumbered down the hill. Bryce had to escape; it would only be a matter of time before the hunter saw him, too. There was no future in being a sitting duck.

He took a deep breath and then he was off, his muscles straining until he ducked behind another wide cottonwood. The hunter, startled perhaps, never fired. Safe for now, Bryce leaned against the trunk while his breaths came out in quick, ragged gasps. He found Preston only a few yards away; he, too, leaned against his tree, but he was freaking, so terrified that his eyes threatened to pop from his skull. Bryce motioned for him to stay calm, but when Preston began to wrap his hand tightly around the pellet gun, Bryce knew it was a lost cause. The idiot actually seemed to be considering shooting back. A pellet gun versus a rifle? What was he thinking?

"Preston, don't do anything stupid," Bryce ordered. "Maybe we'll be all right. I don't think his fat ass can climb down here, and the bullets won't go through the tree. Do you hear me, Preston?"

Preston's response was to cock his weapon. He snarled, spun around, and left the tree. He drew the pellet gun into the air and fired, then spun back behind the cottonwood as if he was in an action movie. He didn't even seem to notice that his shot had missed, that it had sailed over the hunter's head, landing harmlessly somewhere in the woods.

"What are you doing?!" Bryce shouted. "Damn it, Preston!"

Perhaps realizing the stupidity of what he had done, Preston's eyes opened even wider. Words continued to fail him. He choked back bile and felt even more terrified as the fat man shouted.

"I'm gonna kill you sons of bitches!" the hunter barked, followed by a boom and a loud whoosh. More chunks of bark flew from Preston's tree.

Preston, well protected for the moment, took no solace in it. Sanity had left him, and again he slipped into action hero mode. He repeated his earlier maneuver and spun away from the trunk, his gun cocked and ready. He pointed it at the hunter and took aim.

But the hunter was ready. As soon as Preston appeared, another shot boomed. As quick as he had revealed himself, the boy jerked backwards. Cut down, he dropped to the forest floor and writhed in pain.

The hunter crashed through the undergrowth toward them. His gun was pointed outward; it swept the landscape, seeking another victim.

Bryce saw his friend fall, and the hunter charge. He was certain of one thing: he was screwed. "Oh my God."

The hunter's only response was to bring the gun to his shoulder and fire at Bryce.

More bark filled the air, but the tree held. It was only a small comfort. Bryce knew that his hiding place would only delay the inevitable. The hunter would eventually circle around, find him, and shoot him. Distraught, afraid, he held his hand over his mouth, and tried to make sense of the scant choices he had.

He had to run. He had to risk it.

So Bryce did so, weaving in and out of trees, trying to keep them between himself and the hunter. A shot boomed again, missing, but only by inches; leaves rained down overhead. Bryce dared to look back and wished he hadn't, for the sight of the hunter tracking him was terrifying. He watched as the hunter tensed up; Bryce knew he was preparing to fire and did the only thing sensible. He dropped to the forest floor, not breathing again until he heard a bullet whiz overhead. It was strange to feel the force of the slug as it cut through the air. The hairs at the end of his neck stood up, knowing how near death was.

Bryce scrambled back to his feet, knowing it was unlikely he could play that trick again. He wondered how many bullets the gun could carry without reloading. Then again, how many had even been fired? The story problems were over; there were too many variables. Rather, Bryce had moved to English class, a real-life version of "The Most Dangerous Game," the famous story where *man hunted man*. It had been thrust upon him by his English teacher, the same way this hell had been given to him by Preston. Bryce shook his head. The same Preston who now lie on the ground bleeding, easy prey for the predator, as good as dead, if he wasn't already.

Not that Bryce was in better shape. All he could do was run and hope, knowing he couldn't outrun a bullet, and doubting he could out-hope one, either. Still, he had to try. He darted from tree to tree, sprinting, but his eyes stayed behind him, consumed by his pursuer. He tore through the woods until his sneaker caught on a log and sent him sprawling fell face-first into the dirt. He was easy prey, now. It was nearly over; he could only crawl amongst the leaves in a futile and pathetic escape attempt, his legs too weak to stand. Tears streamed down his face. The final shot was coming, it was only a matter of time as the fat man moved toward Bryce like a train, shoving through the brush until he came into a small clearing, a place where he could aim between the trees and get off a clean shot.

Bryce saw the hunter draw the weapon and brace it against his shoulder. The hunter's finger hovered over the trigger. It lingered, extending the agony. Bryce, sobbing, turned toward him and winced. He wanted to apologize, to tell the man that they hadn't intended on smashing his window, that it was only an accident, a stupid mistake, but he knew it wouldn't do any good. He was being chased by a madman. There would be no reasoning. There could only be escape, but first he'd have to reach the Maple tree that stood only yards away. He gave it his all, pushing his body to crawl to it, and to do it fast, but he was so panicked that his body wouldn't obey. He heard the hunter clear his throat and knew the shot was coming. Knowing he was too far away, Bryce stretched . . .

To his great shock, someone was waiting. They stood behind the tree and reached out for Bryce with a broad hand, ready to pull him to safety. Bryce's jaw dropped. He reached for the hand, though he was fighting the urge to turn and run back toward the hunter, for this new man was terrifying, wild-eyed and clad in strange clothes. Yet when the man pulled, Bryce didn't let go, leaving the frying pan to dive headfirst into the fire.

"There you go, you little bastard," the man said in a cracked, haggard voice as he jerked Bryce to safety.

Bryce stared at him with astonishment. The man was clad in a bizarre caricature of formal dress attire, wearing a ragtag top hat, with two feathers sticking out of it, and a shabby leather jacket covered in strange markings and patches. Bryce was reminded of the cheap clowns that would haunt him at parades when he was young.

His skin was a ghostly white, not the peach color of Bryce but a fish belly white. His hair was the same shade, with dreadlocks that sprung out as if they had grown from his hat. His face was spread in a wide grin. Strangest of all, the man, *his rescuer*, Bryce reminded himself, was holding a sickle, which he had leaned against the tree during the rescue. Bryce had never seen anyone like him.

"You're welcome," the man said. "But if you're thinking about running, you might want to think again." As if he had planned it, a shot boomed and whizzed past them. "See?"

"Who are you?" Bryce asked, his voice uneasy. This man had saved him, yes, but he gave Bryce the creeps. There was something twisted, even demented about him.

"Me? I'm nobody," the man said. "Just a regular ole Hummel Park livin', Satan worshippin', Albino colony leadin' hermit." He ran his finger across the blade of the sickle, creating a thin cut that began to bleed. "Pretty sharp. Wanna feel it?"

"Please sir, I'm not here to hurt anyone. Anything you want, I'll do it, just let me go, please!"

The man stared into Bryce's eyes as if he was trying to learn something about him. His eyes were blood red, and manic. "Anything I want, huh? Is that right? What could *you* have that I'd want?" Again he ran his finger across the sickle, considering his next move. "All right. It's your lucky day, cuz I don't want much."

"Anything, sir!"

"Shut up!" the man growled. "Now listen good. You do me one thing— you tell everyone what happened here today, and what's gonna happen, too. You understand?"

"Tell who?"

"*Everyone.* Anyone you meet, you tell 'em. I want everyone to know that this park ain't safe, and that all the legends are true."

"Is that all?" Bryce gasped. He could hardly believe what the man was asking, and yet, somehow he understood.

"No, that ain't all. You better go grab that piece of shit friend of yours. He's bleeding all over my home. And then you better get the fuck outta here. But make sure you come down the front road when you do, boy. I'll explain more then. First, I got some business to tend to."

With that, the man left Bryce behind and jumped out into the woods. He zigged and zagged the same way Bryce had been doing, only he did so with confidence, moving swiftly and powerfully, his heavy steps thudding on the forest floor. Bryce leaned around the trunk to watch, catching only glimpses of his savior as he darted between trees and moved toward the hunter.

The hunter saw him and snarled. "What the hell is this?" He let out a guttural growl, words failing him at the sight of this mysterious man from the woods. When he realized that the man was coming toward him, the hunter pointed his gun and unloaded. But his hands shook terribly, and the shots never came close. Predator had become prey; the hunter could not cope with the strange man turning the tables.

The hunter was quickly out of ammo; the trigger kept clicking while he lost his nerve. He could only watch helplessly as the sharp point of the man's sickle whirled around and knocked the rifle from his hands.

Empty-handed with knuckles bleeding, the hunter turned to run. But he was no longer master of the forest. He tripped and fell, left to balance strangely on his whale-like belly.

"What do you want from me?" he gasped. "Why are you—"

The strange man surrounded the hunter the way Bryce had seen a vulture circle roadkill. He raised the flat end of his sickle, a wooden pole, and brought it down swiftly on the hunter's head.

With the hunter no longer a concern, Bryce turned his attention toward his friend and, perhaps more importantly, to obeying the strange man's orders. He imagined his rescuer was not the type of person who liked to be disobeyed. . . .

He returned to where they had taken cover earlier, fearing the worst. There were no signs of life. What if Preston was dead? Bryce didn't know what he would do. It was horrible, and all because of one stupid decision.

There were chunks of bark and a hole in the tree where the bullet had gone in to confirm he was in the right place. He then found the air rifle, which he stooped to retrieve.

But there was no Preston. Bryce wanted to cry again as his emotions bubbled over and tore through him.

"Psst," came a sound from off to the right of Bryce. "I'm over here."

Bryce's heart leaped; it was Preston! Relief washed over him as his friend emerged from a large clump of brush. His hand was pressed firmly against his shoulder, with blood smeared underneath, but he was alive. Bryce came toward him, staggered by this turn of fortune.

"Preston, are you all right?"

"I'm fine, I think. It only kind of clipped me. See?" He lifted his hand, showing that the bleeding was all but done.

"Holy shit, man, I thought you were dead!"

"Not yet," Preston smiled and pointed up at the man, who now had the hunter bound hand and foot. He was looping another length of rope underneath the hunter's armpits and began to pull him. "Let's follow," Preston suggested.

Bryce felt his stomach lurch. It seemed like a bad idea, and yet, he had been ordered to leave via the road, where he'd receive further instructions. On a morning filled with bad decisions, it never dawned on either of them to stop now.

But the boys kept their distance, going slowly up the staircase as the man lugged the hunter through thick underbrush. They went over the hill and onto the road. Preston winced with every step he took, but insisted he was all right. They continued to follow the strange man, feeling pangs of regret as they walked quietly past the hunter's pickup.

They could hear every grunt and groan as the strange man strained under the hunter's weight. The pavement began to slope downhill, now, and the boys knew they could follow it right out of the park. The man seemed to take no notice of the boys, but that didn't make Bryce any less nervous. "Let's go back into the trees," he suggested. Preston's silent nod told him that he shared his apprehension.

They left the concrete for a small, tree-covered hill that ran parallel to the road, feeling safer until the man began to mutter under his breath. It made them afraid again, for they were peculiar rantings. The curious boys paused to listen until they could clearly hear his craggily voice.

"We finally gonna get our hanging, sweet Hummel," he growled. "They'll talk about it for years, indeed they will. The legend of Hummel Park won't never die! We gone make sure of that!"

The boys looked at each other, their eyebrows rising. They were too frightened to move further. The man continued to rant and rave while the boys waited, listening. The tirade went on for some time, *Hummel this* and *legend that*, growing more frantic until there was a loud crack that ripped through the morning air—the sound of a tree branch breaking. A flock of crows, disturbed by the sound, scattered overhead. The boys watched them glide by ominously.

They stayed where they were among the trees, waiting, though they knew not for what, when suddenly the top hatted man began to sing in a happy tone.

*Ole Catfish got his catch, oh yeah, oh yeah,*
*Ole Catfish got his catch, oh yeah, oh yeah,*
*Done baited his hook and cast his line,*
*Now he and Hummel gone be just fine,*
*Cuz ole Catfish got his catch, oh yeah, oh yeah.*

The tuneless song continued, the lyrics repeating over and over as he marched up the road, jauntily waving his sickle in tandem with his singing.

He went over the hill and his warbling trailed off. The park was silent, now; not even the chirping of a bird or the buzzing of a bee interrupted the quiet, though the boys wished fervently for something to break up the eerie stillness. They stayed put for a good while until they judged things were as safe as they would ever be, and finally left their little place in the woods for the open road. The pavement was narrow, scarcely able to fit two cars, and covered by a thick canopy of trees that leaned over and stretched out above. With their heads turning constantly, they followed the road, feet scuffling as they went quickly downhill. Though they feared what they might find, they didn't dare slow down nor delay.

And then all was revealed.

In the middle of the road lay the fallen tree branch they had heard snap. There were leaves and branches setting in the road at awkward angles.

Underneath the rubble was an orange hunter's vest, with the hefty man wrapped inside. The end of a rope had been pulled tight around his neck, a hangman's noose that had cut deeply into his black skin.

They stared for some time, open-mouthed, and when they finally looked up, they found that the strange man was perched above them, standing behind a tree that was halfway up the hill, with his sickle resting on his left shoulder. He had circled back by walking along the hilltop, unseen and unheard.

It gave them chills to look at him, and only Bryce could find the words to speak. "We won't tell anyone, Mister. Please just let us go. I promise we won't tell a soul."

A wide, toothless grin spread across the man's face. He lowered his sickle slightly from his shoulder, his eyes menacing.

"Wrong. You *better* tell, white boys. You better tell most everyone what you saw. So let me tell you exactly what that was. You tell 'em that you stumbled upon a colony of albinos that was worshipping the devil, and preparing a sacrifice, and then you saw a black man hanging from the trees like the old days! You hear me? You tell everyone you can! And now you get the hell out of here!"

"Yes, sir," Bryce replied. Without another word the two boys dug in their heels and shot down the road. They never looked back, not once, not even when the man decided to shout out one last request.

"And don't you forget about the stairs! You tell 'em you went over and counted 'em, and you tell 'em you came up with different numbers each time you counted 'em, you white bastards!"

**Jeremy Morong** is a writer from Omaha. His first-person tale of killing vampires *The Adventures of Braxton Revere* was released by EAB Publishing in May 2015. His first novel, the adventure-fantasy *On the Backs of Dragons,* was published in 2013. He is currently the Production Manager for the literary journal *Midnight Circus.* He lives with his wife Abby and their two children, who seem to think that Hummel Park has a nice playground. *The Legend of Hummel Park and Other Stories* is his first short-story collection.

**Jill Davis LeBlanc** is an artist and writer who lives with her husband and one very spoiled cat in New Brunswick, Canada—at a safe distance, far, far away from the horrors of Hummel Park! Please visit her art portfolio at http://davisleblanc.weebly.com